# HOUSE on the HILL

# HOUSE on the HILL

JACK HOUSE
in association with
SCOTTISH TELEVISION LTD

RICHARD DREW PUBLISHING LTD.
GLASGOW

Richard Drew Publishing Ltd
The Molendinar Press
20 Park Circus
Glasgow G3 6BE

First Published 1981



HOUSE ON THE HILL is based on a television series devised by Robert Love and made by Scottish Television Ltd for the Independent Television network.

| | |
|---|---|
| Executive Producer: | Robert Love |
| Producer: | Mike Vardy |
| Designers: | Pip Gardner and Peter Alexander |
| Directors: | Mike Vardy and Tina Wakerell |

Made and printed in Great Britain by A. Wheaton & Co Ltd

ISBN 0 904002 54 3 (Cased Edition)

# Contents

DEDICATION

To the authors of the television scripts and to all those in Scottish Television who made this book possible.

# 1878
# The MISTRESS of the HOUSE

# The Mistress of the House · 1878

Glasgow was rich. Glasgow was booming. It was the year 1878 and Glasgow was the Second City of the British Empire – with a population of over one million, one of the biggest cities in the world. In certain circles money seemed to flow like wine – an apposite comparison with the life-style of the Glaswegians who lived on the Hill above the beautiful Kelvingrove Park.

But below all the apparent prosperity of the Second City was a terrible underground – the worst slums in Europe and a degradation so dreadful that one writer described Glasgow as "The Cancer of the Empire". All this was more or less ignored by the rich folk who lived on the Hill in 1878. They had the typical self-satisfaction of the Victorian era, when what was alleged to be respectability was rampant. In those days respectability was encapsulated in the Eleventh Commandment – "Thou shalt not be found out."

From the wide windows of the House on the Hill in Park Terrace there was a wonderful view of the city – the Kelvingrove Park stretching below to typical Victorian tenements of the better sort. Behind that a country hill and, in the distance, the signs of the shipping and shipbuilding on the River Clyde which was the satisfactory indication that the old adage was true – "Glasgow made the Clyde and the Clyde made Glasgow".

Nobody on the Hill seemed to bother about the fact that, within the eight years ending 1865 – a mere 13 years ago – three of the most remarkable murder cases in the world had taken place within the scene which they could see. People still talked about the strange case of the Glasgow fashionable belle of the ball, Miss Madeleine Hamilton Smith, who was charged with the murder of her French lover, Pierre Emile L'Angelier. She was tried at the High Court in Edinburgh and the verdict of the jury was the peculiar Scottish one of "Not Proven", which some cynics say means "Go away and don't do it again"!

Yes, it could be said that nobody on the Hill seemed to bother about the mayhem which had taken place within sight of the Terrace windows, but it's possible that Hester Cooper, as she parted the lace curtains of the drawing room and looked out on to the terrace and the park, did have some sombre thoughts. She had heard a horse and carriage approaching and was anxious to discover whether or not her father had arrived with his new bride.

She was not looking forward to meeting the newly-married pair. She had worshipped her mother, who had died some 15 years before. Since then Hester, now in her late twenties, had looked after her father and run the house in her own fashion. If she had ever had even the remotest sign of a love affair, she had kept it secret. She was not much interested in clothes, although, of course, she went to the most fashionable shops in Sauchiehall Street and Buchanan Street. Everything seemed solid about her father, including the very drawing room from which she was watching the passing carriages. And sometimes she felt that this solidity had been transferred to her. Her only friends were the friends of her father and to them she seemed not only dutiful but subdued and solemn.

At that moment, though, Hester did not feel subdued or solemn. She did not even feel particularly dutiful. After so many years as a widower her father had married an attractive woman young enough to be his daughter. Hester looked across the drawing room to where Henry, the Coopers' butler, was taking down a portrait from above the mantelpiece. Her heart jumped as she saw the picture taken from its rightful place and dumped on the carpet. It was the portrait of her mother and it had hung above the drawing room mantelpiece for as long as she could remember. She loved that portrait as she had loved her mother. But her father had written to say that it should be taken out of the drawing room before he and his bride returned from their honeymoon in Paris.

Henry, in his shirt sleeves and striped apron, looked more like a removal man than a butler. He coughed apologetically as he balanced the portrait in front of him. "It's not them, Miss Hester?" he asked.

Hester shook her head and Henry, knowing that he was committing a crime, blurted, "I didn't think it would be. It's a bit early for the train from London to be in. I'd give them a good hour yet."

Hester said not a word. Her eyes were on the portrait. She looked as if she was about to burst into tears. Henry cleared his throat awkwardly and asked, "Did your father's letter say where he wanted the picture stored?"

It was Hester's turn to gulp. She said wearily, "In the boxroom. Well, for the moment." She looked at her mother again and said, "The room will look empty without it."

Doing his best, Henry tried to be cheerful. "Oh, I'll soon have the other one up in its place," he said.

"That's not what I meant, Henry," reproved Hester.

"No," agreed Henry, and didn't make matters any better by adding, "Though, if you'll allow me to say so,

Miss Hester, it wouldn't just have been right to have your mother's picture on the wall." He swallowed nervously and said lamely, "Well . . . under the circumstances."

"Watching the new mistress of the house?" suggested Hester bitterly.

All Henry wanted to do was to get away. Ever since he'd heard about his master's new wife, he had known that there was going to be trouble.

"Well," he said, "I'll see that Molly gives it a good dusting and I'll wrap it up well in canvas."

He laid the portrait awkwardly against the wall and, instead of his normal butler-like tread, positively scurried out.

Hester sat down and gazed at the picture of her mother for what, she felt, might be the last time. "How I loved her," she thought. "How I still love her."

* * *

Hester was not the only one in Glasgow concerned about the new Mrs. Cooper. There had been all the usual gossip in the West End of the city about the elderly widower taking unto himself a second, and much younger, wife. And particularly interested, naturally, was John Cooper's lawyer, Archibald Maitland. Indeed as Hester stood talking to Henry, Maitland was addressing his handsome son Oliver who had just returned from what in those days was called the "Grand Tour".

"Her name is Laura," said Maitland. "She's English. John told me where from, but I've forgotten."

Oliver looked blank and his father quickly said, "She was an Indian widow, married to an officer in the Gordon Highlanders. Well, he died of malaria and left her with an Army pension – and a gey small one at that."

Oliver laughed. "Wed to John Cooper," he said, "she can use that as pin-money now. What brought her to Glasgow?"

"Oh," said his father, "her in-laws were well-to-do folk from out Balfron way. They offered her bed and board and she accepted, but I got the impression from her telling of it that she was treated more like a member of the domestic staff than a member of the family. Anyway, she left."

Oliver gave his father a mock bow. "An independent spirit, the new Mrs. Cooper. Well, well, who'd have believed it? Seems I can't turn my back for five minutes . . ."

His father broke in. "Five minutes!" he snorted. "Three months! Three bone-idle months squandering your auntie's bequest that I could have invested for you at fifteen per cent."

"It was worth it, Father," cried Oliver, with what was meant to be a gay laugh. "You've often told me yourself that you wished you'd seen more of the world. I simply deferred to your advice. But how did John Cooper come to meet . . . what's her name?"

"The name of the new Mrs. Cooper is Laura, and I hope you'll remember it," said Archie Maitland, who could stand only so much sauce from his son. He allowed the rebuke to sink in and added, "Laura eked out her income by giving private language tuition. John had some notion that Hester would benefit from learning French."

"Oh, come, Father," said Oliver. "Hester has little enough to say in English."

"That's as may be," said Archie Maitland heavily. It wasn't easy to deal with a recalcitrant son. "But let me tell you," he went on, "it wasn't long before Hester's father became smitten with the language lady. Oh, it was all very seemly and they didn't make a big splurge of the wedding." He paused for a moment and then said, a shade reluctantly, "The only blight on the proceedings was Hester. She was very upset and showed it."

"All right," responded Oliver in his easy way, "that's

understandable, I suppose. A good wife can easily turn a man's mind from a diligent daughter."

His father flared at him. "That," he said, "sounds suspiciously like a coarse remark, Oliver."

As casually as if he were brushing off a speck of dust from his jacket, Oliver remarked, "No more than a joke, Father."

Archie Maitland frowned. He said weightily, "John Cooper, in addition to being a valued client, is also an old friend and, as such, not a fit subject for your – arrumph – jokes. When you have more experience, you'll find that folk don't like their lawyers to have a sense of humour. It's not a reassuring characteristic. And, as it happens, you've little enough to laugh at."

Despite his father's attitude, Oliver assumed a superior air. "I hardly see how it affects me," he said loftily.

"All right," said his father. "You must realise that Hester's not the only one who'll benefit from his estate now." He looked directly at his son. "Both her father and me," he said strongly, "entertained certain expectations about you and her."

"Oh," said Oliver off-handedly, "I certainly didn't encourage them. Hester's as sparkling as dill water. After five minutes in her company we run out of conversation and spend the rest of the time in utter silence."

"I've known shakier foundations for matrimony," said Mr. Maitland ponderously.

Oliver laughed. "That sounds suspiciously like a joke, Father," he said.

"Don't be impertinent," said Archie Maitland, but too late.

* * *

The horse and carriage came up the streets from the station. John Cooper sat beside his new wife and admired her. She was stylish, worldly and charming. He was in his sixties and she was still, precariously, in her thirties. He leaned across and squeezed her hand with pride. How lucky his friends in the Royal Exchange would say he was. As for his friends and acquaintances in the West End of Glasgow, their main reaction would be one of envy. He had, he couldn't but admit, one slight worry at the back of his mind. How was his daughter Hester going to behave? She had been a wet blanket at the wedding, and he was afraid that she'd be an even wetter blanket in the House on the Hill.

And, sure enough, there was no sign of Hester as the carriage drove up to Park Terrace. The door was opened by Molly, the young Irish maid. She bobbed a curtsey to the new Mrs. Cooper. Laura walked into her new home. John Cooper was just behind her, his eyes searching for his non-welcoming daughter. Henry, the butler, followed, laden with luggage.

"I hope you had a nice journey, Ma'am," said Molly, with a welcoming smile.

"We did – ah," she said and was prompted by her husband. "Molly," she added, "but it's good to be . . ."

Her voice trailed away and John Cooper behind her said firmly, "Home."

"Yes," said Laura, "home."

Her husband looked round the hall and frowned. "Where's Miss Hester?" he demanded. "Has she gone out?"

Before the servants could reply, he heard the sound of a piano from the drawing room. The music was slow and sad. "This way, my dear," he said to his new wife. "This way, Laura."

Laura's eyes opened wide as she followed him into the drawing room. At once she registered that, though it was expensively furnished, it was a rather ordinary room. Above the mantelpiece, where there should have been something special in the way of pictures – a portrait, perhaps – there was a mundane seascape. On a side table stood a vase of flowers, so badly arranged that Laura shivered inwardly. At the piano sat the girl who was now her stepdaughter – Hester, still finishing her mournful musical welcome.

She played several notes before she seemed to realise that her father and her new stepmother had entered the room. Then she rose from the piano and gave her father what Laura registered as no more than a dutiful kiss.

John Cooper showed more feeling. "Hester, my dear," he said as he kissed her warmly, "I thought you'd be waiting at the door to welcome us."

"I'm glad you're home, Father," was all that Hester said.

Laura, all bright and sparkling, moved towards Hester to kiss her and said, "We have so much to tell you about Paris . . ."

"Really?" said Hester and avoided the proferred kiss. She pointed to the vase of rather sadly arranged flowers. "Mr. Maitland called earlier with these," she said disinterestedly, and added, "They are for Laura."

"That was kind of him," said John Cooper, trying to rescue the situation. "You remember Archie Maitland, Laura – my lawyer – he was at the wedding."

"Yes, of course I do," said Laura. She went over to the vase and inhaled the scent of the flowers. She smiled with appreciation but tweaked at the blooms. "They really are quite lovely," she said. "I'll arrange them properly later."

As she spoke Laura realised her gaffe. At once she turned to Hester and gave her a brilliant smile. "I'm so glad you put them in water," she said.

Hester looked coldly into Laura's eyes. "It was the least I could do," she said stiffly. "The very least."

John Cooper, insulated though he was in Victorian

respectability, realised that all was not well between his daughter and his new wife. He registered a private hope that things would improve by dinner time.

But things did not improve. They all changed for dinner. The first thing Hester noticed when she went into the dining room was the new Mrs. Cooper's dress, straight from their honeymoon in Paris. The second thing she noticed was that Mr. Maitland's vase of flowers had been rearranged to look far more beautiful than her own arrangement. During dinner and afterwards Hester was always polite but it was obvious that she was sulking. Her father, not accustomed to feminine tantrums, did his best to involve Hester in the conversation round the drawing room fire.

"The prices in Paris were outrageous, of course," he proclaimed. "But nothing, I suppose, to what they will be when their Exhibition starts."

Laura, who knew better than anyone else how the conversation was flagging, jumped in. "And there was so much I would have liked to have brought back." John Cooper gave a snort that he hoped would be taken as humorous. "Oh, come now," said Laura. "You can hardly call two gowns extravagant."

John beamed. "Cheap at the price, my dear, when you're wearing them. I'm sure Hester would like to see them tomorrow. Wouldn't you, Hester?"

"If you wish," said Hester listlessly.

The awkward pause was broken when the maid Molly knocked on the drawing room door, entered, bobbed, and said to Laura, "The bed's nice and warm, Ma'am."

Laura, delighted at the interruption, excused herself immediately and bade an apparently fond good night to Hester.

Father and daughter sat in silence for some time and

then John Cooper cleared his throat and said placatingly, "It will take time, my dear. I understand that."

Hester was wilfully obtuse. "What will, Father?" she asked.

"Come, come," said Cooper, "we both know what I'm talking about. Laura isn't your mother and I'm not trying to put her in your mother's place. But I think it's reasonable to expect the two of you to be friends."

"I think I was civil enough to her," said Hester ungraciously.

"Aye," said her father heavily. "As civil as you might be to a passing stranger. But she isn't a stranger. She's my wife and I won't have you forgetting that fact."

Hester broke down and started to sob. "If only I could," she groaned. "Oh, Father, how could you . . .?"

John Cooper, like so many self-reliant men, hated to see a woman in tears. He rose from his armchair and crossed in front of the fire to pat Hester on the shoulder. "Hester, lass," he said, "I stayed faithful to your mother's memory for fifteen years." He sighed. "Maybe that was a mistake," he added.

"What do you mean?" demanded his daughter.

"If I'd remarried when you were younger, still a child," he said with difficulty, "you might have found the situation easier to accept."

"There are some things I can't accept," said Hester bitterly.

Her father tried to laugh it off. "Do you grudge me a little affection and companionship, then?" he asked. "You know, my dear, it's time you thought about such things yourself. There's young Maitland just back from his travels and I fancy he's got an eye for you. With just a wee bit of encouragement . . ."

Hester broke in impulsively. "Oh, Father," she cried,

"don't you realise you've made a fool of yourself? And of me. We're a laughing stock in Glasgow."

"That'll do, Hester," said Cooper sternly.

Hester was releasing her pent-up feelings. "But it's true," she almost shouted. "She's young enough to be your daughter."

"I haven't heard anyone laughing," said Cooper shortly.

"They wouldn't to your face, would they?" asked Hester. "But how can it be otherwise, It's . . . disgusting."

John Cooper paused for a moment. Then he said, "All right, my girl, if that's your attitude. But be clear about this. So long as you're under the same roof that she is, I'll expect – no, I insist – that you treat your stepmother with the respect she's entitled to as my wife. Is that understood?"

Hester realised she had gone too far. "Yes, I understand," she mumbled.

"Good," said her father. "Then there's no more to be said."

* * *

But there was much more to be said. John Cooper, much affected by the traumatic conversation with his daughter, went eventually to see his old friend and adviser. Archie Maitland. The lawyer immediately produced a bottle and poured a glass of sherry for his client.

They'd hardly exchanged civilities before Cooper got to the point. "I never thought I'd find Hester so wilful," he said. "In the past month she's scarcely spoken an unnecessary word to Laura. At her age she should be married and giving me grandchildren to spoil."

"Well," reasoned Maitland, "Hester's eligibility has diminished somewhat now. We're both of us fairly well on in years. Approaching the end of the allotted span, as you might say. If your daughter felt a wee thing insecure . . . well . . ."

Cooper got straight to the point. "You mean when I die, Laura gets my estate," he said bluntly.

"You have an economical way with words, John."

"Not being a member of your profession, Archie, I don't charge them by the yard. And I hope it'll be a while yet before I see the Western Necropolis. Anyway, Laura would see that Hester was taken care of."

The lawyer gave an almost imperceptible shake of his head. "Oh, doubtless. But it would be no more than prudent to set up a trust fund for her. Your wife would hardly object since it's all in the family."

Cooper gave his lawyer a straight look. "And you're thinking it might finish up in yours?" he asked drily.

Maitland laughed. "I wish your ill-natured suspicions were justified," he said smoothly. "But my son Oliver's too fond of his freedom and the lightsome lassies that go with it to think of settling down."

"Well, maybe we can jog his elbow next month," said Cooper with a trace of a smile. "I propose to have a dinner party and you're both invited."

"Showing off the new lady of the house?"

"Just that," said John Cooper. "She's received some of the ladies and been received by others, including – God help her – Mrs. McInstrie who's roped her on to one of her charity committees. But I think it's time she met my friends on a proper social footing. And there's another reason – a remark Hester made." He paused.

"What was that?" asked Maitland.

"Oh, she suggested that some people might find the disparity between my age and Laura's a matter of amusement."

"Ah," Maitland pondered. "And you think they'll feel

less inclined to snigger once they've partaken of your food and drink?"

"If they were sniggering in the first place," said John Cooper, "they won't be after they've met her."

* * *

Hester Cooper had never seen such a handsome man in her life. True, she hadn't had the opportunity of seeing many handsome men. Most of the men she had met were, in her opinion, still boys – and looked like boys. Oliver Maitland, the man she knew her father wanted her to marry, was certainly good-looking in a rather foppish way, but to Hester he seemed to have no character whatever.

Now here, in front of her very eyes, was a fine looking man of character. She mustn't be taken in by his uniform, though. He had arrived unexpectedly and announced himself as Captain Galbraith – David Galbraith. He certainly looked every inch the Captain of a ship – stiff, commanding and serious. He explained that he had just arrived from Australia and had some letters from the Cooper agent in Australia. "I promised to deliver them personally," he said, as if excusing his presence.

Hester felt that no excuse was necessary. "I expect my father home quite soon. Perhaps you would care to wait?"

"If that would be convenient, Miss Cooper. I was hoping to travel to Ayrshire tonight, to spend a few days with my family. I'm reluctant to stay overnight in Glasgow."

"After such a long voyage, that's very understandable, Captain," said Hester. "Would you like some tea while we're waiting?"

By the time tea arrived Hester felt remarkably at ease with this tall, ruggedly handsome man. It was apparent, though, that Captain Galbraith was not accustomed to the niceties of afternoon tea. Obviously a heavy mug would have suited him better than a delicate cup. So she encouraged him to talk about his life at sea, the voyages he had made and the places he had seen. He was a good talker and Hester listened to him avidly. She was sorry when they were interrupted by her father.

"Captain Galbraith?" said John Cooper, shaking hands. "Aye – the Bernera Castle. I heard she'd berthed. You've some cargo for me?"

"I saw to its unloading this morning, Mr. Cooper. I also have some letters for you from Mr. Brown of Sydney."

"Captain Galbraith has been waiting," explained Hester. "He just missed you at your office."

"I took the liberty of bringing them here, sir." The Captain smiled at Hester. "I hardly noticed the time pass."

Cooper's eyebrows lifted a trifle. "Indeed?" he said. "My daughter's been entertaining you?"

"Very well, sir," said Captain Galbraith warmly. He smiled at Hester again and she returned the smile.

"Still," said Cooper, "tea's a wishy-washy sort of hospitality for a sea-faring man. Allow me to offer you something a little more fortifying."

"Thank you, sir," returned the Captain, "but I never touch strong liquors."

"As you wish," said Cooper. He paused for a moment. "Are you in port long?" he asked.

"For several weeks, I'm happy to say. A refit."

"Then you must dine with us some evening," smiled John Cooper.

"Please do," urged Hester. "I would so much like to hear more of your adventures."

Captain Galbraith bowed slightly. "I would look forward to that very much, Miss Cooper," he said. "Goodbye, sir."

"I'll see you out, Captain Galbraith," said Hester, and

as they left the room, John Cooper looked surprised and gave a quizzical smile.

* * *

John Cooper looked at himself in the drawing room mirror and gave his image an approving nod. He was well satisfied with his dinner arrangements. The dinner was for ten people, just a nice number to keep general conversation flowing. He knew Laura was bound to be a success. Maybe her evening dress was a little daring for Glasgow, but she looked wonderful in it. And there was Hester talking to Captain Galbraith, who looked slightly uncomfortable in white tie and tails but was nevertheless bearing up gallantly. Hester? Well, Hester was blossoming. She was still somewhat distant to her stepmother, but John was sure that that would come right. All was going well for the Coopers.

Archie Maitland was also looking over the scene. He could see that Laura had been pinned down by the ineffable Mrs. McInstrie, a terrible woman but important in Glasgow West End society. What, the lawyer wondered, had happened to his son Oliver? It wasn't done to be late for a dinner engagement. He looked round and saw Molly the maid approaching John Cooper. They went out together. Ah, that might be Oliver arriving.

Mrs. McInstrie, in her marked Kelvinside accent, was talking non-stop to Laura. "Of course, my dear," she was saying, "I always say that visiting the homes of these poor unfortunates is the best way of helping them – and it's really become quite fashionable as well. You'll be quite touched by the gratitude they show in return for some wee bit of advice on cookery, or household management or bodily cleanliness. It's very rewarding, I must say."

Archie Maitland saw John Cooper coming into the drawing room with the immensely successful Lewis Potter. So Oliver still hadn't arrived. Maitland lost no time in moving to Cooper's side. "John," he said quietly, "I think your wife needs rescuing from the dreaded Mrs. McInstrie." Cooper led his newly arrived guest straight to Laura. "Let me introduce you to Mr. Lewis Potter," he said.

"Oh, do excuse me, Mrs. McInstrie," she said and could hardly hide the relief on her face. "I'm so glad you could accept, Mr Potter."

Lewis Potter was a small man but had immense presence. His teeth showed between his moustache and beard and he said, "It's a great pleasure to meet you, Mrs. Cooper, and one I've been looking forward to. What a charming home you have."

John Cooper's eyes rested fondly on his wife. "A home's what she's made it," he said. "For too many years it was just a house."

"Just the man you want to see, Laura," said Maitland's voice beside them. He turned to Lewis Potter. "I should warn you, sir, that tonight's dinner, excellent as it may be, will cost you a pretty penny. I'm down five guineas myself already."

"Shame on you, Mr. Maitland," cried Laura. "Why should Mr. Potter feel anxious?"

"Because," said Maitland, looking mock serious, "he is a director of the City of Glasgow Bank and as such controls an untold fortune."

Potter, looking like a cat which had licked the cream, said, "But not within my own gift, I'm afraid."

Laura laughed. "Mr. Maitland is just teasing me because I've been soliciting subscriptions for a little charity I'm connected with."

"Ah, I see," said Potter. "Well, the depositors' money is sacrosanct but I daresay I can manage a few private guineas."

Maitland pulled out his watch and looked at it. "You're

doing well, Laura," he said, "and you could raise more by levying a fine on late-comers."

By the drawing room door Hester was in deep conversation with Captain Galbraith. There was one particular thing she wanted to know about him.

"And did you find your family well, Captain?" she asked.

"In the best of spirits," replied Galbraith. "My mother and sister Jenny are anxious to spoil me, I'm afraid."

"You're not married, Captain?"

"No, ma'am. A sailor's life is hardly attractive to those left on shore."

"When do you sail next?"

"Next Wednesday, if all goes well."

Hester tried to conceal her disappointment. "So soon?" she said.

And at that moment the door opened and Oliver Maitland was shown in. "Good evening, Hester," he smiled. "How very pretty you look."

Hester had hardly time to introduce Oliver to Captain Galbraith before Archie Maitland approached. "So you've finally decided to show up, Oliver," he said reprovingly. "Punctuality is the courtesy of kings – and dinner guests."

"I'm sorry, Father," said Oliver easily. "Some urgent business came up –"

"Make your apologies to our hostess," said Maitland and took him over to Laura. "This is my late and reprehensible son, Oliver."

Laura looked at the almost-too-handsome young man and the sight pleased her. "Mrs. Cooper," said Oliver, clearly captivated.

"Laura," she said.

"Please accept my apologies for my late arrival," blurted Oliver.

"They aren't necessary. Your father is in a teasing mood this evening."

John Cooper broke in with a laugh. "He's already teased Mr. Potter out of a handsome donation to Laura's charity."

"Ah, I didn't say handsome," protested Potter. "Not handsome."

Maitland was not to be diverted. "But substantial just the same, eh?" he said. "As substantial as your new premises in Buchanan Street. Business must be good."

Potter smiled deprecatingly. "I think I can say that the bank's ventures are prospering, even though world trade has slackened somewhat." He turned to his host. "We look to the future, Mr. Cooper. Our most recent investments have been in Australia. Land shares. The country's expanding all the time."

"Captain Galbraith was saying as much," returned John Cooper. "He's not long back from Sydney. You might be interested in having a talk with him."

Laura took Oliver's arm and gently guided him away. "Oh, dear," she sighed, "and I did ask John to keep any business conversation to the port decanter. But I'm forgetting – you are a man of affairs yourself, Mr. Maitland."

"I will become my father's partner next year," said Oliver. "And if I am to address you as Laura, I insist that you call me Oliver."

"As you wish. Tell me – Oliver – the urgent business that made you late . . . Was she pretty? Now, no prevarications – your reputation has preceded you."

Oliver laughed. "My father has been engaging in some slander. Well, I won't lie to you. At this time of the year, the West End Park is very pretty. I went for a walk by the Kelvin and misjudged the time."

Dinner was announced and, as the guests walked across

the hall to the dining room, Oliver offered Laura his arm and in they went.

John Cooper grew more and more complacent as he looked round the table. Laura was the perfect hostess and she excelled at keeping the conversation going. Even Hester seemed to be sparkling, but then she was sitting beside Captain Galbraith.

As the guests were leaving, Archie Maitland came up to John Cooper and said, "A splendid affair, John. An occasion to be remembered – as it will be, together with its hostess."

"I think it had the desired effect," said Cooper with a satisfied smile.

Captain Galbraith and Oliver Maitland were out in the hall, just ready to leave. "We hope to see you again, Captain," said Laura. "And you will call into my offices before you sail?" asked Cooper.

"I won't forget, sir," replied Galbraith. "Nor will I forget my promise to you, Miss Cooper."

He was hardly out of the door when the inquisitive Archie Maitland said, "And hat's all this about promises?"

Hester flushed slightly. "Captain Galbraith has said he will write descriptive letters from all the places he visits."

"That should be most instructive," said Maitland. "Oliver, I can offer you room in my carriage."

"Thank you," said his son, "but it's such a pleasant night I think I'll walk."

"By the Kelvin?" said Laura.

"Not tonight. Perhaps tomorrow morning. Goodnight, Laura."

Laura went back into the drawing room. In a moment her husband came in and kissed her. "That was a triumph," he exulted. "You excelled yourself."

"I think it was a successful evening," said Laura.

"More than that. You charmed the whole occasion. But you've had an exhausting day."

"I am a little tired," she confessed.

"Then I suggest you spoil yourself and sleep late tomorrow."

"Nonsense," laughed Laura. "I'll be fully recovered by the morning. In fact, I think I shall go for a bracing walk in the park. I'm told that it's very pretty at this time of the year."

* * *

Laura was as good as her word. The very next morning she went down the hill from the house into the West End Park. She had seen the River Kelvin running through it, but only from the windows. Now she walked slowly beside it. She had to make several perambulations before she saw Oliver Maitland. It was, she felt, a meeting of lovers. He seemed to respond as she did. They had just reached the eastern end of the park when Oliver said, "I live in a flat quite near here. Would you like to see it?"

"Of course I would," responded Laura warmly. Once there, it seemed natural to her that they should make love. She hardly gave a thought to her elderly husband. They agreed to meet again – "As often as possible," said Oliver eagerly. Laura was just as eager. She would have to think up excuses for being out of the house, but that shouldn't be difficult. John Cooper was at work all day. He did not even come home for lunch. She could be out shopping. She could be out visiting. And, praise be to Mrs. McInstrie, she had a perfect excuse in her charity work.

Oliver was an ardent lover. Her husband knew nothing and she kept him happy. All was for the best in the best of all possible worlds. Laura's only worry was Hester. She had known right from their first meeting that Hester resented her. But what could Hester do?

And that was the problem which faced Hester too. The

euphoria of the dinner and of the unspoken but clear relationship between herself and Captain David Galbraith had lessened, although she was delighted to get a letter from the Captain each time he arrived in one of his foreign ports. Her feelings for her stepmother had once again become bitter. She had a feeling that something unusual was happening in Laura's life. She was out so often during the week and when she came home in time to supervise dinner, she had a buoyant, almost defiant, gaiety.

Then there came the afternoon when Hester decided to go to a string quartet recital in the Botanic Gardens. It was a pleasant day and the walk from the house to the Gardens was not far. She walked up to the Kibble Palace, the enormous glasshouse where the event was taking place. By the time she arrived she could see that the recital had already started. She hesitated, wondering whether to wait until that piece of music ended. And, as she looked through the glass pane, she saw Laura. Her stepmother seemed to be paying no attention to the music. A man's hand was possessively over hers and she was absorbed in him. Hester couldn't see who the man was because one of the many palms in the palace hid him from view.

What should Hester do? She felt she should not go into the recital and spy on Laura. And yet there was her father to consider. As she gazed unbelievingly through the window she saw the man's other hand come round Laura's waist. Hester had seen enough. She turned and walked back home, her mind sorely troubled.

Some days later she was writing a letter to Captain Galbraith when the maid entered with a letter for Laura from Mrs. McInstrie. "Mrs. Cooper is out just now," Hester said. "Just leave it on the mantelpiece." She returned to her own letter, then stopped writing and on an impulse went to the mantelpiece and examined Mrs.

McInstrie's letter. The flap of the envelope was only lightly stuck down. She hesitated for a moment, then flicked it open and read the letter.

Soon afterwards her father came home. She saw with concern that he looked ill and tired. "Where's Laura?" he asked.

"She went out an hour ago," said Hester. "To Mrs. McInstrie's."

"Oh, that woman and her charity meetings," said Cooper. "She's taking up far too much of Laura's time."

"She won't today. Her maid brought a note round to say that the meeting's been cancelled. Mrs. McInstrie has a sore throat."

"Why do you make that remark in such a peculiar way?" asked her father.

Hester couldn't stand it any longer. "Laura's being unfaithful to you," she blurted.

John Cooper was outraged at the accusation. Realising she must continue, Hester said, "She is having an association with another man. I don't know who he is, but on the day I saw them together she was supposed to be at one of her charity meetings. Why don't you ask her where she's been today?"

And so, when Laura came home, he did. At first she prevaricated and then, when he told her he knew about Mrs. McInstrie's letter, she changed her story. She said she had walked in the park for an hour and then, on impulse, taken a train to Largs. Pressed further, she admitted that she was seeing another man. It was a purely platonic affair, she claimed, with a friend of her former husband's.

"Do you want a divorce?" she asked.

"No," he said. "I won't bring scandal on the house by divorcing you. It goes without saying that you will never see him again."

"I promise," said Laura.

"No promises. I'm not asking for your word because I don't attach any importance to it. But I'm telling you beyond any possibility of misunderstanding that, if I so much as suspect that the affair hasn't ended, nothing will stop me from putting you through that door and into the street with no more than the clothes you stand up in. Is that clear?"

Laura nodded.

"Good," said Cooper. "You'll have time to move your things into another bedroom before supper."

The following morning he met his lawyer, Archie Maitland, and handed him a letter instructing him that the Cooper property should be put into a trust fund for Hester while he was still alive. A mere pittance would be left to Laura. "And I want your solemn word, Archie, that this matter will remain confidential between us."

"You have it," Maitland assured him. But, of course, he had to discuss the matter with his son Oliver, whom he had recently taken into partnership. He couldn't know that Oliver was Laura's lover. He saw no relationship between his son and his client's wife other than normal friendliness. Oliver lost no time in explaining the true situation to Laura. She realised how serious things were. Unless she acted swiftly and ruthlessly she would be left with nothing – except Oliver.

Things came to a head quite unexpectedly. Captain Galbraith returned from Australia, bearing another package of letters from Sydney to John Cooper. He also asked Cooper if he could have his daughter's hand in marriage. Cooper hummed and hawed and said, "We'll see," but he gave his permission to the Captain to take Hester to the new Gilbert and Sullivan opera at the Theatre Royal.

Left alone in his study John Cooper felt old and tired. But he had business to do. His old friend, Archie Maitland, couldn't be with him that night, but he was sending his son Oliver to attend to the matter. When he arrived they discussed the buying of a new warehouse, and then suddenly Cooper asked the young man to pour him a glass of brandy. "Are you feeling ill, sir?" asked Oliver in concern.

Cooper swallowed some of the brandy, grimaced and said, "Oh, just a touch of heartburn. Hardly surprising, what with one thing and another. I've had some alarming news about the City of Glasgow Bank. I asked my Australian agent to enquire into their investments and his report is far from encouraging. The trouble is that I hold substantial shares in the bank myself. I want them sold as quickly as possible."

Oliver cleared his throat. "There is another matter outstanding," he said. "The question of your estate and Hester's trust fund."

Cooper produced a legal document. "Here it is," he said. "I signed it yesterday. I need two witnesses. You can be one. The second's a most appropriate choice." He pushed the document across his desk. "If you would," he said to Oliver.

As Oliver signed the will, Cooper crossed the room and opened the door. "Ah, I thought I heard you, Laura," he said. "Would you join us for a moment? I'd like your assistance with a legal matter. I need your signature as a witness."

Laura entered the study. She looked at Oliver, whose countenance was ashen. She saw the will on the desk with his signature as a witness. Her husband handed her the pen.

"Put your name there," he said. "Just beside Oliver's."

"No," said Laura.

"Why not?" asked Cooper and, receiving no reply, said, "I asked you why not?"

Laura looked her husband straight in the eye. She said softly, "You evil, spiteful old man. Do you think I don't know what this is?"

"You shouldn't," said Cooper. "But clearly you do." He turned to Oliver. "How does this come about?"

Oliver attempted to bluster. "I felt obliged to inform Laura of the substance . . ." His bluster faded away.

"Did you now?" said Cooper. "Why?"

"It . . . it was the only honourable thing to do."

"Honourable!" said Cooper harshly. "When did you inform her? Where did you inform her? What chance did you have to inform her?"

"We met privately," started Oliver unhappily, but Laura cut him short. "Tell him the truth, Oliver," she said and, as her husband turned to her with dawning comprehension on his face, she said brutally, "Yes, we are lovers! We have been for months. That's the truth!"

Cooper turned to Oliver again. "My God," he cried. "You! The thought never crossed my mind."

Laura's voice was hard. "Did you think you could marry a wife half your age – expect her to grace your house and your bed – live with your dreary daughter and be content with that?"

"Laura, for God's sake!" implored Oliver.

John Cooper's face was suffused with rage. He raised his hand to strike Oliver, then suddenly staggered and clutched at his desk. Oliver caught him and tried to hold him up. "Take your hands off me!" roared Cooper. "Don't touch me – don't touch me –"

He collapsed back into his chair, trying to say more, but his voice tailed off into a series of agonising gasps.

"He's having a stroke," cried Oliver. "Send for a doctor!"

Laura said calmly, "We are the only ones in the house."

"Then I'll go," said Oliver.

"No!" Laura was still calm. She took him by the arm and half shoved him from the study to the front door. "Go home, Oliver," she said to her lover.

"But he's – he's dying," said Oliver.

Laura opened the door and pushed him out. "You weren't here this evening," she said.

She went back to the study. John Cooper was lying slumped across his desk, with the will still under his hands. He was dead. Laura steeled herself and pulled the piece of paper away. Her impulse was to burn it, but the fire was unlit. Her eye fell on the book-cases which lined the room and she went over, selected a book of the right size and put the will between its leaves.

* * *

Oliver Maitland was seeing a new Laura – one who was a consummate actress. She played the part of a brave widow and looked very fetching in black. Her story was a simple, straightforward one. Her husband had been alone when he died. He had gone to his study after dinner to examine some papers from Sydney which Captain Galbraith had brought that afternoon. He had asked not to be disturbed and as usual she had respected his wish. She had waited up until Hester returned from the visit to the Theatre Royal with Captain Galbraith, and then they both had gone to bed. Owing to John's poor health they were occupying separate rooms so she hadn't known that anything was wrong until the morning, when Molly had come to tell her that John was dead at his desk. She had discovered the body when she went into the study to tidy up.

It had been dreadful, Laura said, to think that she had been in the drawing room, just across the hall from the study, and had not known that he was dying.

She was assured by all who heard her story that she couldn't possibly blame herself. The doctor had said that John Cooper had died of a sudden stroke, so there was nothing that she could have done anyway. Laura responded to these assurances with a brave but sad little smile.

With Oliver. however, she was quite different. "The papers are hidden in one of the book-cases in the study," she explained. "I'll destroy them and Hester will never know."

"Don't you feel any guilt, Laura?" Oliver asked her.

"I'm sorry he died as he did," she said in a matter-of-fact tone, "but I've never been able to afford guilt. What prospects did I have before I married him? A position as a governess or a companion – a slightly superior servant working for bed and board and enough money to buy one decent dress a year. And what prospects did he have? A few years of lonely existence. Instead he had my company and my body."

"Don't talk like that!" exclaimed Oliver.

Laura gave him an indulgent smile. "You don't face facts, Oliver. No, I don't feel guilty. I feel that I'm entitled to security and happiness. I have the first as his widow. In time, I'll have the second as your wife."

They were in Oliver's bedroom and she was already undressed. Oliver, unhappy and out of his depth, said, "You're forgetting about Hester."

"No," said Laura, still smiling. "I'm not." She went to him and started to unknot his tie.

Hester had not forgotten about Laura either, although she was altogether more concerned with Captain David Galbraith. He came to see her and give her the unwelcome information that he would be sailing in three or four days. He hoped that their correspondence would continue.

"Of course," said Hester. "And when you have time to reply, perhaps you could send your letters to me care of Mr. Maitland."

"Certainly," said the Captain. "May I ask why?"

"I'll be leaving this house soon," explained Hester. "A personal matter. I can't stay here. I feel like an unwanted stranger. And I have a small income, sufficient for my needs."

"I see," though the Captain's voice didn't sound as if he saw. He paused. "Miss Cooper . . . May I address you as Hester?"

"Yes," breathed Hester. She was sure she knew what was coming. Archie Maitland had shown her a letter he had found among her father's papers. It was from Captain Galbraith asking John Cooper's permission to pay court to his daughter with a view to matrimony. The lawyer had thought that, as it concerned her, she should read it.

David Galbraith made heavy weather of his proposal. And, in true Victorian fashion, he ended, "May I inquire if my offer of matrimony has any hope of success?"

"The prospect pleases me more than I can say," replied Hester. "I would be most happy to marry you, David. Just one question – do you love me, David?"

"Didn't I say so?" asked Galbraith incredulously.

"No," said Hester.

"With all my heart," said the gallant Captain, taking Hester into his arms and kissing her with some vigour.

When they had recovered, they planned the wedding for early in October, when he would be back from his coming voyage. And he suggested that, since she was leaving Park Terrace, she might consider staying with his mother and sister at their Ayrshire home. Hester said she would be delighted.

She lost no time in telling Laura of her decisions – to leave the house and to get married in October. Laura, since the death of her husband, had ceased to conceal her animosity towards Hester. She made the customary noises but it was clear that she welcomed Hester's departure. She even did all in her power to hasten it. So Hester left the House on the Hill, as she thought, for ever.

* * *

On the second of October, 1878, the day after Captain David Galbraith and Miss Hester Cooper were wed in Ayr, the City of Glasgow Bank went bust.

Archie Maitland was sitting in his office reading the "Glasgow Herald". Oliver was lounging opposite him. "For some time past," Maitland read to his son from the newspaper, "rumours have been in circulation unfavourable to the position of the bank, and these have been only too well founded . . ." He looked up. "I'm damned if I heard any rumours," he said.

"It was pandemonium outside their head office when I passed," said Oliver. "The police could hardly control the crowd and there was talk of arrests."

"Aye," said Maitland grimly, "and the board of directors will be among the first. Potter's for the high jump, that's a certainty. God knows how many they've ruined with their irresponsibility. I must find out more about this affair."

He rose and put on his coat.

"We aren't at risk, are we?" asked Oliver.

"No, but some of our clients are. The ones who have shares in the bank."

"They'll hardly be ruined," said Oliver off-handedly.

His father glared at him. "They might be, you gomeril!" he barked. "It wasn't a limited liability company!"

It took most of the day for Archie Maitland to discover all the facts about the bank crash. They were even worse than he expected. In the early evening he went to the House on the Hill to see Laura.

The lawyer did not beat about the bush. "I'm the bearer of very bad news, I'm afraid," he said. "You'll be aware that the City Bank ceased trading this morning?"

"I've heard talk of little else," replied Laura. "But I don't see how it concerns me. I have no funds in that bank."

"You have shares. A substantial number – and you've been listed in the press."

For the first time Laura was alarmed. "Listed?" she asked.

"As a shareholder, and therefore a debtor. The bank's gone down with more than six million pounds of the depositors' money. They'll want it back from the shareholders."

"I don't understand," said Laura, bewildered. "How much do I owe?"

Maitland paused. "I estimate your present liability at ten thousand pounds as things stand at the moment. But it could be much, much more."

"These shares," said Laura. "How do I come to have them?"

"Your late husband bought them on the advice of his good friend, Mr. Lewis Potter. As John's widow, you inherited them. You should know the worst, Laura. There are only fourteen hundred shareholders, small people for the most part and not wealthy enough to meet the claims of the liquidators. Half of them would go bankrupt at the first call and then the debt would transfer to those who remained. Only next time, it wouldn't be five hundred pounds. It would be double that because there would be fewer people able to pay. And so on. You could be wiped out, lose everything."

Laura made her mind up in an instant. She crossed from the drawing room to the study, went to the book-case and took out the book with the will in it. Then signed her name as a witness beside Oliver's signature.

She took the will back to Maitland and said, "Here is

John's will. It proves that the shares belong to Hester."

Stern-faced, Maitland looked at the document and handed it back to Laura. "Aye," he said, "the signatures are genuine. Though yours is scarcely dry."

The drawing room door opened and Oliver walked in. He started when he saw his father with Laura. His eyebrows went up as he looked at her and then, as he saw the will in her hands, he visibly wilted.

"Come in, man," said his father harshly. "You're expected and you know the way well enough."

"I'm sorry, Oliver," said Laura. "I had no choice but to tell your father everything."

"Aye, she told me," said Maitland. "God, when I look at you, I feel sick. Taking John Cooper's wife for your mistress. Well, are you too ashamed to speak? That might be something."

"I – I love Laura," stammered Oliver. "We intend to get married."

"Do you now? Well, I hope you enjoy each other's company. You'll enjoy little else. The liquidators'll see to that."

"I don't own the shares," protested Laura. "You said yourself that the will was in order –"

"Oh, aye," said Maitland sardonically, "signed, witnessed and perfectly legal. He transferred the shares to Hester – but you forget they were never registered in her name. You're still liable, Mrs. Cooper. Is that not so, Oliver?"

Oliver nodded glumly.

"Take on this woman and you take on everything that goes with her. And if this will ever sees the light of day, if any word of it gets out, you're finished! Disgraced! Struck off! D'ye hear me?"

Oliver, speechless, nodded again.

"And frankly," said Maitland, "I don't think this bitch

would hesitate for one single second to use it if she thought it was to her advantage. However, since my own good name's involved, I'll stand by you as best I can, providing – but only providing – that you leave this house with me tonight and never see this woman again."

"And what if he doesn't?" demanded Laura.

"If he makes his own bed, he can lie in it. Though, if it's your bed, he'll likely find he's sharing it with others." He turned to Oliver. "I'll wait for you in the hall," he said and walked out.

Laura went to Oliver and put her arms round his neck. "Darling," she said, "it won't be as bad as he says."

"It could be," said Oliver. "Laura, I have to think."

"About what?" asked Laura. "Even if I lose everything, we can still get married."

"But Laura, as your husband I'd be responsible for the debts. It could go on for years! They'd keep coming back for more."

"Oliver, what are you saying?"

"I have to think, Laura – I have to think."

He took her arms from his neck and hurried to the door. "Oliver!" cried Laura. Oliver stopped and turned round. She had the incriminating document in her hand. He held his breath. "I'll never see you again, will I?" she asked. Oliver did not say a word. "Just remember one thing," she said, "I loved you."

She tore the will in two and threw it on to the fire. For a moment Oliver hesitated, then went out and closed the door behind him.

* * *

The House on the Hill was empty. From the drawing room window Laura watched the last of the furnishings being piled into the removal van. She lifted her small suitcase and walked into the hall. She shivered as she looked round the emptiness. The only object left was a large canvas-wrapped painting.

"Well, that's the last load, Mrs. Cooper," said the head of the removal men, as he came in the front door.

"Yes," said Laura softly. "It's all gone."

The removal man was embarrassed. "Aye, I'm afraid so," he said. "City Bank, was it? The wife's sister lost her savings – it was only fifty pounds but it was a' she had."

"She'll get something back," Laura said. "They're paying seventeen shillings in the pound.

The removal man looked at her suitcase. "There's room for you and the case on the van if you're going in our direction," he offered.

"Thank you," smiled Laura. "But I can get a tram at the foot of the hill to the Central Station, and my case isn't heavy."

The removal man turned away and Laura, seeing the canvas parcel, called after him, "You've left something behind."

"Oh, that," he said. "No, somebody bought that privately from the liquidators. It's being collected later."

He undid the canvas and the portrait of Hester's mother was revealed.

"Is the purchaser's name on the label?" Laura asked.

A voice behind her said, "Yes, it is." Laura turned to see Hester standing in the doorway. She looked at Laura levelly. "Mrs. David Galbraith, Girvan, Ayrshire."

Laura said not a word. She smiled wryly, picked up her suitcase and walked out of the house. Hester watched the trim, defeated figure walking down the hill. She had a sudden impulse to run after Laura and make her peace. Then she turned and saw the portrait of her mother and stayed where she was.

# 1909
# MAN of STRAW

# Man of Straw · 1909

The House on the Hill seemed empty. In one of the windows was a sign saying "For Sale". But inside the house was the new purchaser, Andrew Douglas. The windows were still shuttered and Andrew had meant to take down the sign. He hoped his wife Emily hadn't noticed that he had forgotten to remove it. She was already making a tour of the place to make sure it was worthy of their son.

With some difficulty Andrew opened the shutters of one of the windows in the drawing room, peered outside and removed the offending sign. He felt a proud, proud man. Why shouldn't he? He was a successful shipbuilder in the world centre of shipbuilding – the River Clyde. All the shipbuilding yards from just below the Broomielaw right down to Port Glasgow on the Firth of Clyde were booming. "Clyde-built" was a famous slogan world-wide. Even in the United States the shipbuilders could not compete with the Clyde.

It was 1909. King Edward the Seventh was on the throne. The Liberal Government were in power, although something called the Labour Party were challenging them. They hadn't much hope, in Andrew Douglas's opinion. Especially as one of the leading Liberal M.P.s was his only son, Rupert. He'd bought the house for his son. Since Rupert became a Member of Parliament – what was it? Yes, nearly five years ago – they had hardly seen him. Now he'd written to say that he wanted a Glasgow base and Andrew was delighted to have found and bought one. Inwardly he thought that Rupert's wish for a Glasgow home had something to do with the fact that a General Election was looming. But, after all, what was wrong with that? The important thing was that he was going to be back in Glasgow.

From somewhere upstairs his wife's voice reached him. "Andrew!" he heard her cry. He went out into the hall and Emily came down the stairs from the first floor. "Ah, there you are," she said. He noted how immaculate she looked against the bare surroundings. Ah, well, Rupert would no doubt have the place looking spick and span in no time at all. But where wasRupert? He should have arrived in Park Terrace by this time.

"Will it do, do you suppose?" asked Emily, gesturing around her.

"It will," said Andrew and added positively, "It'll have to. But Rupert should have been here by now."

Emily said anxiously, "It'll be the railways, I expect. Not his fault at all. How much I'm looking forward to seeing him again."

Andrew nodded and decided to unshutter more windows. It would make the house look better. He was interrupted by Emily's cry. "Andrew – where are you? He's here!"

He felt as tense and excited as she did, but he concealed it. He went downstairs, took Emily's hands and said, "Shall we let him in, do you think?"

He grinned and went to the door. A hansom cab was just driving away as he opened the door. He saw his son and – to his astonishment – a woman with him. A secretary, maybe?

"Hello, mother," said Rupert, and they embraced.

"Five years," said Emily. "They kept you from us for five years." She did not look at the woman.

"Aileen," said Rupert, and the woman moved to his side.

"I'd like you to meet my mother, Aileen," Rupert went on. "And my father."

They shook hands with this unexpected stranger. Rupert said smoothly, "Aileen and I were married ten days ago, Father. I'd like you to meet Mrs. Rupert Douglas."

Emily's eyes widened. She looked as if she was about to burst into tears. Aileen was worried. She had told Rupert that the news of their marriage should not be sprung on his father and mother. They should have been told. Now they both looked shocked, though they quickly started making noises of congratulation.

* * *

From the house in Park Terrace Rupert and Aileen were taken to the Douglas home, not far away, to stay until the new place was furnished. But Andrew lost no time in taking his son to his club – the Western, the oldest in Glasgow. They sat in a quiet corner and a waiter brought them a couple of brandies.

Andrew Douglas cleared his throat and said suddenly, "What's all this tomfoolery, Rupert?"

"I'm not sure, Father," replied Rupert easily, "quite what you mean by tomfoolery."

"It was a wicked thing to spring it on your mother like that," Andrew was emphatic. "And are there no Glasgow lasses good enough for you?"

"I'm sure there are," Rupert seemed in command of the situation. "But I was in London. I needed a wife and so I took one."

Andrew was shocked. "Needed a wife?" he said incredulously.

Rupert was patient. "Westminster's a peculiar place, Father. Fashions change but politicians remain the same. It was Leon Campbell – my agent, you know – who made the suggestion. 'Study the careers of the great Parliamentarians,' he said. 'Almost without exception their public lives were supported by a contented home life'."

"And you married for that reason only?" asked his father.

"That," answered Rupert, "and the fact that sooner or later – and the later the better – women will have the vote. When that happens any bachelor past forty will need to look to his laurels."

"Is that how you see yourself, Rupert? A great man?"

"I've come so far, and done well enough."

"But suddenly you're afraid?" asked Andrew directly.

Rupert laughed. "There you go with your shipyard logic! It's a purely commercial instinct to confuse expedience with fear."

"I've found the two things usually walk side by side," said his father shortly.

"Then in this case you're wrong." Rupert was still in command of the situation. "Shortly before he became ill the late Prime Minister told me that I was marked down to take over the Home Office."

Andrew Douglas snorted. "Nothing that Campbell-Bannerman did would surprise me!"

"Granted," laughed Rupert. "And now I'm afraid that Asquith, our new P.M., has his own favourites. I'm being overtaken – passed by in favour of a generation of whippersnappers."

"And Asquith has a mistrust of bachelors?"

"Not precisely." Rupert sipped his brandy.

"Then why do you need a wife so suddenly?" demanded Andrew.

"Oh, did I not tell you? Aileen is related to Asquith. On the Scottish side of his family, incidentally, which won't come amiss at the next election."

Andrew Douglas couldn't believe that his son was saying these words. Rupert did not seem to notice his father's shaken look. "Not closely related, you understand. I mean, no dowry to speak of. But he's devoted to her."

"So," said Andrew, "that's your recipe for a happy marriage, eh?"

"Oh, don't be naive, Father," said Rupert. "A good marriage, I'll grant you, is a possibility. But a 'happy' one? Do you know of many?"

Andrew looked at his son. "A few," he said.

"Few indeed," said Rupert complacently. "Well, I'll settle for a contented one – and for men like us, success and contentment *do* march side by side."

* * *

At last the House on the Hill was ready for Rupert and Aileen Douglas. It had been decorated in the very latest Edwardian style. Rupert was delighted with it. He even remembered to thank his father for all that he had done. And Aileen had settled down. She and his mother had hit it off right away. Indeed, Aileen seemed to get on well with everyone she met, including Leon Campbell, his redoubtable agent. Although Rupert had a high opinion of himself, he did admit that he owed something to the advice which Leon gave him. Indeed, he reflected, Leon had never been wrong yet. Leon had suggested a house warming party when Rupert and Aileen had settled down. "But Aileen knows no one to invite," said Rupert. "Leave it to me," said Leon confidently. "You fix the date and I'll fix the guest list."

And now the house warming was in full swing. Rupert

and Aileen were in conversation with the family physician, Dr. Carson, but Rupert was only half-listening. He was intent on examining his guests. Leon Campbell had invited some people who were hardly known to Rupert, but, since Leon was on the ground in Glasgow, and he had been away from the city for five years, he trusted Leon's judgment. There was just one visitor who worried him a little. He was a dark, rather saturnine young man and Leon had introduced him as McGregor, a Glasgow journalist. Rupert could not put his finger on it but something about McGregor made him feel uneasy.

Dr. Carson was telling Aileen that he had once met Mr. Asquith, the new Prime Minister. "Must be what?" he said. "Oh, at least two years ago. A fine man – a gentleman."

"He's always been a good friend to me," said Aileen.

"And he'll be a fine P.M. too," smiled Carson. "Given the chance." He turned to Rupert. "And once he learns how to pick his first team, eh, Rupert?"

Rupert disengaged his attention from the menacing McGregor. "Oh, there'll be a shake-up once the election's over and won," he said confidently. "My time will come, doctor."

He was not the only person observing McGregor. Leon Campbell was watching the journalist too, and beginning to regret that he had invited him to the party. He saw McGregor moving closer to Rupert and excused himself from the group he was with.

Dr. Carson was saying, "And you've been up here how long this time, Rupert – six weeks or is it seven?"

"Almost eight," said Rupert.

McGregor suddenly materialised beside him. "Have you not been missed at Westminster, sir?" he asked.

Rupert started but recovered quickly. "With a General Election in the wind," he answered, "I'm sure I'm not alone in thinking it's more important to hold my seat than it is to occupy it."

They all laughed, except McGregor. "But you will be returning for the Budget debate?" he asked.

Leon Campbell was right behind him. "If it's an interview you're after, McGregor," said Leon, "I suggest some other place."

"Or at least a more convenient time," put in Aileen.

McGregor was not a whit abashed. "I would appreciate a few words, sir," he said, in what for him was almost a placatory tone.

"Oh, very well," said Rupert. "You never know – and only a fool plays games with the all powerful Press." He led the way to his study.

Aileen turned to Leon. "Mr. Campbell," she said, "will my husband be leaving for Westminster?"

"I think he should," replied Leon.

"Will he take me with him?" she asked.

"I doubt it, ma'am."

"Why not?" demanded Aileen.

"He's been away a long time. His enemies will be watching – hoping that he's been distracted by his marriage."

"Enemies?" repeated Aileen incredulously.

"They breed on success like flies. Rupert must prove that his mind is still concentrated – and that he bears no ill-will at being passed over for office."

Before Aileen could reply, her mother-in-law bore down upon them. "Isn't it wonderful, my dear?" she cried. "All these people – important people and Rupert the grandest of them all. You must be very proud!"

Leon chose the moment to bow politely and leave the two ladies. He wanted to know what was happening between Rupert and McGregor. There was no one in the hall and he walked upstairs to Rupert's study. He stood outside the door listening intently.

Inside, behind an impressive desk, Rupert was lounging in his swivel chair. He had not offered McGregor a seat, but the earnest newspaperman did not appear to have noticed the slight.

"In Glasgow," he was saying, "we have the worst slum concentration in Europe."

"I'm aware of it," said Rupert.

"And now," McGregor went on, "just when the money's been found to do something positive, this Liberal budget threatens to ruin the whole thing."

Rupert shook his head. "Are you naive enough to suppose that this proposed Hyndland development scheme is in any way philanthropic?"

"Your new Land Tax will kill the plan stone dead," returned McGregor.

"So? It'll be the Tory speculators and developers who feel the pinch."

McGregor was persistent. "And the people in the slums? People dying every day? From cold, from dirt and disease."

"Believe me, McGregor, those people are more scared of facing a radical change in their lives than they are of sharing an outside tap or toilet seat."

"You don't even want to help them?" demanded McGregor.

"Helping those who don't seek your help can be a dangerous game."

"But worth the risk, Mr. Douglas."

Rupert waved a languid hand. "Then let the new Socialists take that risk, McGregor. I stand behind my party – security, familiarity and prosperity." He shifted in his seat. "McGregor," he said solemnly, "there's talk of a war in Europe – just talk as yet – and rumour, but rumour taken very seriously. Fighting a war, if it can be avoided, is plain foolishness. But preparing for war spells prosperity.

"Aye," said McGregor, "but for who?"

"I'm talking about votes," said Rupert patiently. "The poor-vote. Those people you profess to be bleeding for. I'll tell you what they want, McGregor – pennies in their pockets, coal on their fires, beer in their bellies, and sheets on their bed. Given those things – I'm telling you – it'll be a brave man who tries to tear down the tenements."

Leon Campbell, listening outside the door, had heard enough. He entered the study quietly. The two contestants didn't even know he was there.

"You're good, Douglas, I grant," grated McGregor. "But you're wrong. You're talking about votes – I'm talking about lives, and souls."

Rupert was still at ease. "I respect your motives, if not your manners, McGregor. We'll speak again – but after the election."

"Assuming that you're re-elected," said McGregor rudely.

"Yes, of course," said Rupert smiling. "Assuming that."

Leon Campbell could not wait any longer. "McGregor," he said.

McGregor turned in surprise.

"Mr. Douglas has guests waiting," said Leon.

McGregor shook his head impatiently. "One more thing," he said.

Rupert gave a weary assent, and McGregor immediately broke in. "You served on the Cable Landing Rights Committee?"

"Correct," said Rupert.

"Which recommended state ownership of the new wireless telegraphy system proposed by the Marconi Company?"

Rupert, looking puzzled, said "Yes?"

"That decision," said McGregor, "is worth a great deal of money – a fortune, in fact."

"A necessary investment," said Rupert.

"Aye, but who'll reap the profits? Will you answer that?"

Rupert, for the first time in this unfortunate interview, was confused. But he rallied and said, "The people, of course – through the Post Office – your slum dwellers amongst them."

McGregor sneered. "They might get to lick at the saucer," he said, "but it's you and your high-minded friends who'll be after the cream, I'm thinking. Good night, Mr. Douglas."

Leon Campbell opened the study door for him and out he went.

Rupert looked at Leon and said, "The man's mad, I tell you – or some kind of a crank at the best."

"There have been rumours," said Leon cautiously.

"As with any progressive step," began Rupert, when Aileen came in. Rupert rose awkwardly. "I'm sorry," he said.

"People are leaving," explained Aileen.

"Of course," said Rupert and went downstairs.

"Who was that angry little man, Leon?" asked Aileen. "He pushed right past me."

"Oh, just a local do-gooder," said Leon. "Nothing to worry about. Shall we go down?"

But Aileen was still worried when the party was over and she and Rupert were going to bed.

"You don't blame me?" she asked.

"For what?" Rupert returned.

"For keeping you here," said Aileen.

"I chose to stay," said Rupert. "Until the house was ready. My own idea."

"To be with me?" asked Aileen. Rupert looked somewhat nonplussed, then gave a smile and a nod.

"Suppose you've missed out, dear? Lost a great opportunity?"

"Oh, they'd know where to find me," said Rupert.

"I was talking to Leon Campbell about your leaving for London. He'd do anything to help you, wouldn't he?"

"We have been friends for a long time."

She moved closer to him. "Rupert," she said, "I want to be of help too."

Rupert looked puzzled. "In what way?" he asked.

"Really help," said Aileen. "With your work."

Rupert smiled. "You know my views on women in politics," he said.

"Not all men think like you do." responded Aileen.

"Meaning Leon?" he asked, and Aileen nodded. "Leon would find a use for anyone – if he thought they could help the party."

"Even me?" asked Aileen. "That's right. It's his job – rounding up the faithful. Wives are very important to Leon."

"But not to you?" asked Aileen.

He held his arms out to her and they embraced.

* * *

The election was on. Rupert Douglas kept moving constantly between Glasgow and London. Leon Campbell held the fort in Glasgow. Rupert's study had been turned into the campaign headquarters. The walls were plastered with posters advising the electors to vote Liberal and for Rupert Douglas. Aileen had become the chief typist. But this day Leon saw her suddenly stop typing and put her hand to her head.

He went over to her desk. "Are you all right?" he asked.

"Yes, of course," replied Aileen. "Just tired."

"Dr. Carson said that you weren't to do too much."

"He's an old worrit," laughed Aileen.

Leon did not respond. He said, "Rupert still doesn't know? About the baby."

Aileen smiled. "It's not the kind of thing a man should learn from a letter, Leon," she said. "I'll tell him myself as soon as he comes home."

But Rupert Douglas had been in London for three months. True, he kept writing and sometimes he telephoned but this could not make up for his absence.

Dr. Carson was Aileen's most frequent visitor. "Every confinement carries a certain element of risk," he told her.

"Because I'm past thirty and this child is my first?"

"I don't want you to be alarmed," the doctor said. "Just take care. When's Rupert due?"

"Tomorrow," said Aileen happily.

She was at the Central Station to meet him as the train steamed in. How handsome and powerful he looked, she thought, as he walked along the platform. They got into the wating car and, to her disappointment, his opening remarks were about politics. He gave her a perfunctory kiss, asked how she was without waiting for a reply, and said, "If you ask me, young Churchill and Lloyd George have the old man running around in circles. All they talk about is war – build up our defences, more guns, more ships, spend, spend, spend."

"You think they're wrong?"

"Not the point." Rupert shook his head. "If there is a war and Winston's proved right, there'll be no holding him."

"Is it likely?" said Aileen.

"Lord knows. The Kaiser's holding the Balkans to our throats with a bayonet. The Socialists are preaching revolution as the one chance of salvation for the working man. Anything might happen. Only one thing's certain – we must win this election. And it'll be close – damn close."

He took Aileen's hand in his and said, "I'll need every ounce that you or anyone else can give me."

As the car moved smoothly along Park Terrace they were surprised to see a crowd outside their house. Obviously they were there to greet the returning M.P., although there was a group of suffragettes marching up and down with placards saying "Votes for Women." Reporters and photographers were there too. Among them Rupert could see the familiar figure of McGregor. They got out of the car and posed for a photograph. Leon Campbell already had the door open. The newspapermen called for an interview.

"Later, gentlemen, if you don't mind," said Rupert affably. "It's been a long journey, and a longer time since I was with my family. If you'll excuse me . . ."

McGregor shouted, "One thing, Mr. Douglas," but Leon Campbell closed the door in his face.

* * *

Leon Campbell was worried – not only because of the problems of the election campaign, but also because Aileen had not told Rupert that she was bearing his child. Leon knew, and both Andrew and Emily new, but Rupert never seemed to notice his wife's condition. His mind was totally devoted to the election. He toured the constituency, making speeches, chucking babies under the chin, talking to anyone who might vote for him. Aileen faithfully accompanied him. It was important that he should be seen with his wife.

There came the day when the results of the election were announced. Leon Campbell had the champagne ready. Rupert Douglas was in by a good majority. Aileen held up her glass towards Rupert and suddenly fainted.

They took her back to the House on the Hill and put her to bed. Outside the house a crowd had gathered, shouting to the new M.P. to make an appearance. But the new M.P. did not want to appear. He had just learned that his wife was about to have a baby and he was angry. He paced up and down in the drawing room, and his father and Leon sat and watched him.

"Why didn't she tell me?" he demanded.

"She wanted to be at your side," said Leon.

"How will it look?" cried Rupert. "Dragging her around like some useful kind of ornament when all the time . . . what will McGregor make of that if he gets wind of it?"

"Is the look of the thing the issue, Rupert?" asked his father.

"No, of course not," returned Rupert. "But all the same – imagine if it had happened sooner, during the campaign. What was she thinking of?"

Leon Campbell said, "She said nothing out of love for you."

"I had a right to know," Rupert proclaimed. "It's my child too. And what will her family say? Her friends in London – if anything happens?"

"The truth can't bring you any discredit, Rupert," said Andrew Douglas.

"The truth?" repeated Rupert.

"You acted in ignorance," said his father, "and she out of love."

"And what kind of man does that make me?" demanded Rupert. "Not to know – to notice? What kind of husband? Do you know what they'll say? Behind my back, of course. They'll say she was afraid to tell me."

He was so caught up in his own affairs that he hadn't seen his mother come into the room.

She had heard him and said, "Nonsense."

"How is she?" Leon asked.

"As well as can be expected," said Emily.

"And the child?"

"Holding on."

"Thank God!" said Rupert.

"She'd like to see you," said Emily.

"Yes, of course." Rupert moved to the window and looked out. "Get rid of them, will you, Leon? Say that their clatter is disturbing my wife – anything. It'll look bad if I do it."

"Leave them to me," said Leon.

And, as Rupert went upstairs, father, mother and agent exchanged embarrassed looks. As he went up, Rupert met Dr. Carson. "She'll be all right, doctor?" he asked.

"They both will – with a little care," said Carson.

"Good," said the preoccupied Rupert. "You'd do best to leave by the back way."

"Very well," said the doctor. "And by the way – congratulations."

"Thank you," said Rupert modestly. "It was a fine result."

"It's not the election I was referring to," said Dr. Carson. "Good night."

Rupert was taken aback for the moment. Then he went to the bedroom door. Aileen heard her husband's approach. She struggled up into a sitting position, hoping she looked better than she felt. Rupert came in, looking concerned. But she could tell, as usual, that he was concerned for himself – not for her.

"You should have told me," he said reprovingly.

"I'm sorry."

"We could have lost everything," he said.

Aileen was hurt to the roots of her being, but she said nothing.

"Of course, it has to stop," Rupert went on. "You understand that? I've told Leon."

She nodded. "I daresay the child – when it comes – will

provide you with a more suitable employment." He frowned.

"Rupert," said Aileen pleadingly, "aren't you pleased? Even a little?"

He paused, then smiled. "Yes, yes, of course. Well, I've things to do. I'll see you later. Work, you know."

As he went out, Aileen sank back against the pillows and gave way to tears.

* * *

His father, his mother and his wife were all there to see Rupert Douglas off to London. Leon Campbell, as ever, was there too.

"I'll be home as often as my duties allow," said Rupert, a shade awkwardly.

"But you will be home for . . ." Aileen hesitated. "In the summer when the baby's due?"

"It would take an army to stop me," said Rupert convincingly. He looked at Leon who had told him that the reporter McGregor seemed still to be a menace. "Forget about McGregor, Leon," he said. "Public life is plagued by lies and innuendo. Just watch my back for me while I'm gone."

He bade his goodbyes and went.

In London he moved easily into the pattern of Parliament. But he did not forget Aileen. And there was a constant nag in his mind about the egregious McGregor. The weeks went by and it was time to leave London and go back for the birth of his boy – he was sure it would be a boy. As his train moved into the Glasgow Central Station he engaged a porter to take his luggage and, as he approached the barrier, there was Leon Campbell waving a newspaper to attract his attention. "Always faithful, ever sure," quoted Rupert to himself. But when he reached Leon he had some unpleasant news. The headline of the newspaper read, "Marconi Scandal, Enquiry Opened."

In the limousine purring up to the House on the Hill, Leon asked, "Is it all as bad as McGregor makes out?"

"Worse," said Rupert. "A watershed. If the whole of the Cabinet are involved – and that's the way it's beginning to look – it'll mean ruin for some and advancement for others, and change the whole political spectrum."

"That may not be all bad," said Leon shrewdly.

"We can't afford it, Leon – an upheaval on this scale at Westminster with the Kaiser still rattling his sabre in the Balkans." He permitted himself a wintry smile. "You know it's rumoured that the whole affair is a deep German plot to ruin the Government."

He handed the newspaper back to Leon, who said abruptly, "You've not asked after Aileen."

"What?" said Rupert, nonplussed.

"Your wife, remember?" said Leon drily.

Rupert recovered himself. "How could I forget?" he exclaimed. "She writes every day – sometimes twice. It may be a good thing when she has a child to occupy her time."

"She's missed you a great deal," Leon pointed out.

"Do I sense a rebuke?"

"It's been three months," said Leon.

Rupert shook his head. "It was impossible, Leon. The King's death – this Marconi business. Had it been at all possible, believe me, I'd have been back sooner."

The limousine slowed gently to a halt outside the House on the Hill. And there was Aileen opening the front door. She rushed into Rupert's arms. They kissed and then he held her at arms length. "You look well," he said, almost enthusiastically for him. "No, you look better than that – wonderful! It must be something that agrees with you."

"And you, Rupert?" asked Aileen. "Are you all right? Really all right?"

"Never better. Why? Who's been spreading rumours about me this time?"

"No one," Aileen assured him. "I was afraid you might be ill."

"Not even that excuse, I'm afraid," said Rupert, almost tenderly.

"You don't need an excuse, Rupert," said Aileen. "Ever!" Rupert didn't quite know how to respond. Aileen seized his arm. "Come upstairs," she cried. "You must do that first – see the new nursery. We have everything ready."

"Everything ready?" Rupert actually laughed. "So soon?"

They kept laughing as they mounted the stairs to the nursery.

* * *

Rupert was back in the Western Club. Leon had told him that a reception for him had been arranged, a formal dinner. He'd drawn up a rough draft of a speech, based on the fact that the third great Glasgow Exhibition was to take place next year, in 1911. "The Exhibition Planning Committee will all be there," he had said. "They'll welcome your interest and advice."

Rupert was now in mid-speech. He looked round the prosperous and successful Glaswegians and went on, "And we should centre the whole Exhibition around two main themes – Glasgow's glorious history, and Glasgow's glorious future."

His audience applauded. "A custom-built Palace of History," he continued, "with exhibits collected from all parts of Scotland – all parts of the world."

The applause broke out again. "So much for our history," said Rupert. "And our future – well, there can't be any doubt about that. Our future lies on the banks of the Clyde. Our future is safe in the knowledge of our world renown as the builders of mighty ships of war!" For a second or two he was distracted because he thought he saw the worrying McGregor coming in at the back of the dining room. He rushed on, "To bring home to Mr. Churchill and his friends at the Admiralty the full truth of our potential, while I instruct our Cabinet of the full urgency of our city's needs."

As the club members started to cheer and rose to their feet, Leon saw his opportunity. He jumped up and held his glass aloft. "Gentlemen," he shouted. "To the future of our city – the Second City of the Empire."

The guests seized their glasses and drank. At that moment the thought of McGregor became a reality to Rupert. There he was, as out of place as usual. Heads turned as McGregor shouted, "Mr. Douglas!"

Rupert looked round to Leon for help. "Not now, McGregor," remonstrated Leon. But McGregor waved his newspaper in their faces. "You either hear it now," he was still shouting, "or read it over breakfast in the morning."

"Hear what?" demanded Rupert. The audience were angry at the interruption. There were shouts of "Throw the bounder out!"

McGregor ignored them. He read from his newspaper, "The personal interests which undeniably exist between certain members of the Government and the Board of Marconi cannot be in the public interest . . ."

"That's a libellous statement, McGregor," Rupert was calm but forceful. "The Enquiry's just opened."

"You don't deny that the terms of the contract awarded to the Marconi Company are more than generous?"

"The terms are fair," said Rupert.

McGregor swept on. "Or that considerable fortunes

have been made by share speculators – many of them directly involved in these secret negotiations?"

"Which is why the Home Secretary has ordered the Enquiry," answered Rupert, still patient in the face of this inquisition.

McGregor raised his newspaper again and read, "One reason that this barefaced swindle will go through is that we have, as yet, in this country no method of punishing those men who are guilty."

Rupert lost his patience. "None of this is new. It's muck-raking and speculation."

"Then we'll come to what may be news," said McGregor, a note of triumph in his voice. "You served on the Committee which recommended the terms of the Marconi contract, did you not?"

"That's not news – it's public knowledge."

McGregor paused. He knew that the audience were all against him, and yet were hanging on his every word. He said deliberately, "What is not quite such public knowledge is that during the negotiations your father, Andrew Douglas, shipbuilder, bought several thousand shares in Marconi, sold them when they were at their height, then when rumours that the negotiations had collapsed caused the shares to crash, he reinvested."

There was complete silence in the dining room. "Now," McGregor went on, "thanks to the favourable terms of the contract – your contract, Mr. Douglas, drawn up by your Committee, these shares are on the up and up again. Your father stands to make a second fortune."

There were murmurs but Rupert stood his ground. "I have never," he said, "at any time or in any circumstances had any interest in Marconi Telegraph shares. Nor have I had any communication with any person other than my immediate colleagues at Westminster regarding such an interest. Any man who says different is a liar and a slanderer. If you print otherwise, McGregor, you are a liar, a slanderer – and a coward."

McGregor was not to be moved. "But it is true, is it not, Mr. Douglas, that you are in anticipation of what is called in refined circles, a 'Happy Event'?"

This change of tack puzzled Rupert. He nodded. McGregor went straight on. "Which is perhaps why, Mr. Douglas, we find you skulking here in Glasgow. Out of sight out of mind of the Committee of Enquiry? Is that the idea? Or do they already know in London that there are three thousand Marconi shares at this very moment held in trust for a child as yet unborn? Your child, Mr. Douglas."

Rupert was so stunned that he sat down abruptly. He looked along to Leon Campbell for some kind of assurance but there was a blank look on his agent's face. Rupert had the uncomfortable thought that Leon seemed almost to be enjoying the scene. The guests were rising and throwing angry questions at McGregor and, more hurtfully, at himself.

It was the same when they got back to his father's house. Leon was quite detached as the furious Rupert, knowing by now that his father had bought the Marconi shares, demanded an explanation.

Very much on the defensive Andrew Douglas muttered that it was a gift. "And what's wrong in that?" he added.

"What about your own investments?" asked Rupert.

"Any fool with half an eye can see that telegraphy's the coming thing," answered Andrew reasonably.

Rupert was not prepared to be reasonable. "The biggest witch-hunt in history is under way at Westminster."

"All right," said Andrew. "Tell this so-called enquiry the simple truth. Scottish businessmen aren't known to be wanting, you know. I don't know how slow on the uptake they may be in London, but up here every man with wherewithal's been at it. Where's the harm?"

"And this trust fund? That's true as well?"

"And why not?" Andrew was fighting back. "A proud grandfather to be making provision in anticipation. It's not unusual. Just a wee present, that's all."

Rupert pulled himself together. "Father," he said more calmly, "the people have been swindled and they want heads to roll. You, with your 'wee present' have handed them mine on a plate." He turned to Leon. "I'll have to resign, of course."

"Will the Prime Minister accept your resignation?" asked Leon.

"He'll not have a choice," said Rupert firmly.

"What will you do – if you resign, I mean?"

"I've no idea." Rupert shook his head at Leon. "I hadn't exactly planned all this, you know."

"I still think you're making a mountain out of a molehill." Andrew shook his head. "But if you're set on giving up politics, there'll always be a place alongside of me, in the shipyard. That's what I've wanted for years – Andrew Douglas *and Son*. It has a fine ring to it."

Leon broke in. "And with your contacts at Whitehall," he said to Rupert, "you'd have first bite at every contract the Government tendered. And if there's a war . . ."

Rupert looked at Leon, then at his father. He almost suspected that he was being manoeuvred, but he was accustomed to doing the manoeuvres and found it hard to believe. "You know, Father," he said, "if I didn't know you better . . ."

His father could not conceal his delight. "So what do you say?"

"I'll think about it," replied Rupert and, as he walked out, his father and Leon exchanged smiles of congratulation.

* * *

Rupert's resignation was accepted by Mr. Asquith. Aileen did her best to comfort him, for he was taking the situation very badly. She was surprised one morning when he called to her from his study. He was sitting at his desk reading the letters which had just arrived. "Perhaps that would interest you," he said, handing her the one he had opened a moment before. She saw at once that it was from the Prime Minister. "We have great need of men like you in the Upper Chamber," she read incredulously. "Men with experience of Government, loyalty, integrity and discretion." He was asking Rupert to accept a peerage.

"Wonderful!" she cried. "It's a fine, generous letter. You will accept?"

"I see no alternative," Rupert said, a thought sourly.

"And we can go back to London?"

"No," said Rupert decisively. "Asquith's new Liberal Peers are ten a penny there. At least here in Glasgow a title may still have some meaning."

"Lord and Lady Rupert Douglas!" Aileen clasped her hands in delight. "Will our son be an Honourable?"

Rupert gave a condescending smile and turned to his next letter. His expression changed as he read it.

"What's the matter?" asked Aileen.

"Letter from the local Party Headquarters," said Rupert shortly. "Asking me to endorse their new choice of candidate."

"And who've they chosen?"

"Leon Campbell," said Rupert and looked out over the park with hurt eyes.

By this time he was already a director of his father's shipbuilding firm and he made this an excuse for not helping Leon Campbell during the election. He did contribute to the Party's election fund but he refused to appear on the hustings. Nonetheless, when his former agent asked for advice, he gave it freely. And he was pleased, for the sake of the Liberal cause, when Campbell won, albeit with a lower majority than Rupert's. He and his father were in the Club when Leon made his triumphal entry. Rupert registered the fact that it was not so very long ago that the triumphal entry had been his own.

"Congratulations," Rupert said to Leon, a slight tinge of sarcasm in his voice. "You know, I suppose, how much I envy you?"

"Envy? Between friends?" Leon paused for a moment. "We are still friends, Rupert?"

Rupert shook hands warmly and asked Leon to join them. Over the brandy old Andrew Douglas lost no time in putting Leon in his place, an old Scottish custom. "We've a new order from Austria," he said triumphantly, "signed and sealed. Two new Dreadnoughts. Envy that, Mr. New Member of Parliament."

Leon turned to Rupert. "How's Aileen?" he asked.

"Arranging tea parties and opening garden fetes. Lady Douglas is very popular."

"I hope she's not overdoing it," said Leon.

"Don't worry. I make a dutiful consort, and Dr. Carson hovers like a mother hen."

"Dutiful consort be blowed!" snorted Leon. "You're doing a grand job, Rupert. You'll end up Lord Provost yet."

"I'd hoped for Lord Chancellor," said Rupert.

"Don't let him fool you," said Andrew. "You're looking at a happy man. A man with a future."

"But with the best of it behind him!" Rupert's smile concealed his bitterness and they laughed.

"Are things really so bleak, Rupert?" rallied Leon. "I'd say that you have a great deal to look forward to. Don't you realise how much it is that *I* envy you?"

Rupert was thoughtful as he left the Western Club and

went home. Aileen, now eight months pregnant, was preparing for bed when he walked into the room and kissed her with more feeling than he had shown for some time.

"I've just left Leon at the Club," he told her.

"Leon?" repeated a delighted Aileen. "You mean you're friends again?"

"I should never have doubted him. For the first time in weeks I feel alive – with something to look forward to?"

"All thanks to Leon?" asked Aileen.

"No, thanks to you. But it took Leon to make me see it."

"See what?"

"That a peerage is a fine thing to have achieved – when you have a son to carry the title on." Aileen's delighted expression changed to one of apprehension. "To be someone, to build a fortune – useless ambitions until a man has a son. That is something worth working for."

"Leon said all that?"

"Not in those words, perhaps – but he made me see that I have a future worth fighting for. Where I failed – my son will succeed. It's so obvious. He'll do everything I dreamed of doing."

Aileen was frightened by his intensity but she had to speak. "Rupert," she said, "we may not have a son."

"But we've always talked about 'he' – taken it for granted. If you want something, Aileen, want it badly enough, it happens. You won't let me down, will you? I don't think I could stand it. We must have a son."

Dr. Carson was horrified when Aileen told him how Rupert had demanded a son. "The man's mad," he said, "and by God I intend to tell him so!"

But he did not get a chance to tell him. Aileen's birth pangs came all of a sudden. Rupert sat in the study drinking brandy, listening for sounds from the bedroom. He had sent a message to Leon Campbell, and it was nearing midnight when Leon arrived. He poured a glass of brandy for his friend, whose first question was, "What does Carson say?"

"It's premature, of course," shrugged Rupert, "but apparently that's not unusual with a first child." He handed the brandy to Leon. "When do you leave for London?"

"As soon as I know that . . . that everything's all right."

Rupert held up his glass. "Well – shall we drink to him?"

"Him?" repeated Leon.

"What else?" said Rupert confidently.

They sat and waited – and waited. Rupert dozed off but Leon listened vigilantly. Just as the study clock chimed four he heard the first cry of a new born baby. "Rupert!" he cried. Rupert woke, looked round to get his bearings, then jumped to his feet. The study door opened and in came Dr. Carson, in his shirt sleeves and looking exhausted.

"How is he?" Rupert spoke hoarsely.

" 'He'," said Carson slowly, "is a small but perfectly healthy baby girl. Congratulations, Rupert."

Rupert stared at the doctor in disbelief. It was Leon who asked, "And Aileen?"

"Very weak, I'm afraid. Very ill." The doctor turned to Rupert. "She's asking for you."

Rupert went to the bedroom. Aileen, very pale and still, watched her husband anxiously. He looked at her and tried to speak, but the words wouldn't come. He sank down on to a bedside chair, staring into nothingness.

Aileen looked at him for a long moment but his expression told her that her worst fears had come true. She turned her face to the wall.

Aileen did not last the day. When Rupert was told that she was dead, he didn't seem to realise what had happened. He was still locked in his own disappointment.

* * *

Rupert did not see Leon Campbell again until the day of Aileen's funeral. Once the coffin had been lowered into the grave, Rupert said, "Do you agree with Carson, Leon? And the others? That I could have saved her?" Leon shook his head. "Oh, no one's said it," Rupert went on, "but it's what they're all thinking."

"They'll soon come round," said Leon.

"They're wrong, of course," Rupert was trying to convince himself. "There was nothing I could have done."

"What will you do now?" asked Leon.

Rupert shrugged. "Go back to London. Start again. If there is a war, and it seems likely, there's sure to be some sort of job for me." He paused. "You were very fond of her, weren't you, Leon?"

Leon nodded. "And those shares – the Marconi shares – the trust fund. That was all your idea?" Leon nodded again. "Because you felt that I was neglecting my wife?"

"No," said Leon abruptly. "Don't lay the blame at Aileen's door, Rupert. What I did, I did for the Party – not for her. I'll say goodbye."

"Shall I see you in London?" asked Rupert.

Leon was already walking away. "I think it rather unlikely," he flung over his shoulder, "don't you?"

Rupert Douglas could not bear to stay in Glasgow a moment longer than absolutely necessary. He asked his father to sell the House on the Hill and the day came when he stood on the steps bidding goodbye to Andrew and Emily.

"You'll let me know when you've sold the house?" he asked Andrew.

"Then you'll not be back?" said Andrew.

"I don't know yet," replied Rupert.

"And the baby?" asked Emily. "Flora? You'll send for her?"

"London – with a war in the air? It's no place for a child. She'll do better with you."

He shook hands with his father and made to kiss his mother. Emily turned her cheek. Rupert shrugged. "Goodbye, Mother," he said and walked down the steps to the waiting Argyll. As the car drew away, Andrew turned and locked the door of the House on the Hill. Then he offered his arm to Emily and they walked off in the opposite direction.

# 1918
# SEMPER
# FIDELIS

# Semper Fidelis · 1918

It should have been a happy time for Elsie. Here she was, ensconced in a great big terrace house overlooking Kelvingrove Park. It was the beginning of November, 1918, and after what some people called Armageddon and others the Great War, a lot of people were saying optimistically that the fighting would soon be over. If that was true, Elsie would be one of the happiest women in the world.

But she had other things to think about. Here she was, living in the basement of this rather down-at-heel mansion, with a man who was not her husband and a twelve-year old boy who had got hold of her heart as no other person had ever done. "David!" she said aloud, as she thought of him. There was, of course, another person she thought she loved – the tall, decisive, handsome Jack Bonfield. She had met him in Edinburgh, in one of the pubs in Bohemian Rose Street. She was a country girl who yearned to be a dancer on the stage, but she had found that, even in Cosmopolitan Edinburgh, there were not many opportunities for expectant dancers. There were, however, a number of opportunities for expectant young girls – as long as they were not too expectant.

Truth to tell, and Elsie admitted it to herself, she was in

danger of becoming a prostitute. She had discovered, from one or two experiences, that what she had been told was a Fate Worse Than Death could actually be quite pleasant. But all her country upbringing was against that. She felt ashamed of herself and yet she had to live. So, when she met the masterful Jack Bonfield, not long invalided out of the Army, and he suggested, quite delicately, that she should join him in Glasgow, where he had a lovely house, she accepted.

She was amazed at this House on the Hill. Although the interior was now down-at-heel, it had obviously been a very fine place indeed. Jack explained that it belonged to a family called Murray-McNeil. He had been butler to Sir Archie Murray-McNeil, who went to war in August, 1914. Bonfield immediately followed him. He believed in the family motto – "Semper Fidelis" – "Always Faithful," Jack kindly explained to Elsie. And so the two of them went to France. Captain Sir Archie Murray-McNeil wanted to get out of the country anyway. His wife had discovered that he had had a son by another woman. The best way to avoid such trouble was to go and fight for your country. But Sir Archie, as it turned out, died for his country in No Man's Land in France. The faithful Bonfield was badly wounded and so sent home.

As some returning heroes found, he was given a job right away. Lady Murray-McNeil, living in her Highland fastness, asked him to take on his old job in the Glasgow house and keep it in trim until she decided what to do with it. What Lady Murray-McNeil did not know was that Jack Bonfield had promised his Captain that, if anything untoward happened, he would look after young David. Always faithful, he kept his word. And that was how young David, the twelve-year old son of the Captain, was in the house.

Elsie knew that, according to the kirk way she was

brought up, she was Living In Sin. But that didn't worry her too much. She felt she had a husband and a son and she lavished love on both of them. The real worry was Bonfield's regular habit of dressing up in Sir Archie's Black Watch uniforms. A big wardrobe held them and Bonfield couldn't keep away from it. His delight, when it came to supper-time, was to change into the Officers' Mess magnificence of the Black Watch. And Elsie had to admit that he looked every inch an officer in the red jacket with gold trimmings and the dark tartan trews. But she couldn't help feeling that it was wrong to wear someone else's clothes.

She was at the front of the house and heard his steady step outside. She peered through the lace curtain and there he was – the perfect officer in his Glengarry, khaki jacket and trews, swinging along with a conquering air. Out on the terrace a passing soldier saluted him and he returned the salute with an officer's customary condescending air. She vanished down into the basement.

Bonfield's conquering air deserted him as he came through the front door. He saw a letter on the floor and picked it up apprehensively. He looked furtive as he went into the drawing room and gazed up and down the terrace. There was no one about. He felt in his uniform pockets and brought out four pounds and some documents. One of the documents was an identity book. He flicked it open and looked at the front page.

He read, "Surname: Semple. Christian names: Ewan Robertson. Officer's No., 27482. Rank: Captain, War Substantive. Regiment: Black Watch. Next of Kin: Mother, Mrs. J. Semple, 22 Skelmorlie Avenue, Glasgow."

Jack Bonfield was a man who tried to suppress his emotions, but what could have been taken for a guilty expression crossed his face. He put the identity book back in his pocket, looked at the four pounds and stowed away two of them, and then called, "Elsie!"

She appeared at the drawing room with remarkable promptitude. Had she been watching him? He gave her one of his big smiles, handed her the money and said, "Two pound. Don't spend it all in the one shop. A good feed for three the night. Officers' meat, and bread and butter coupons in lieu of provision."

"Nothing else you want, sir?" said Elsie sarcastically.

"Later, Elsie, later," Bonfield kissed her but she did not respond. "Your passion overwhelms me," he said. Then asked, "Where's the lad?"

"In the garden," Elsie answered, nodding towards the dining room.

Bonfield marched across to the dining room. There was young David at the garden wall, being talked to by the girl next door. Bonfield was a great man for the quotations. "Himself the primrose path of dalliance treads," he uttered.

"It's her's doing the dallying," replied Elsie, matter of factly.

"Jealous, are you?" rallied Bonfield, then once again looked worried. "I've mislaid my wallet."

"Again? Really, Jack, you're all over the place. Your master must've taken more care of you than you of him."

"Not as well as you do," said Bonfield absently, for he was now opening the letter he'd found on the mat.

He scanned it and looked up. "What date's this?" he asked.

Most people who are asked suddenly for the day's date are taken aback. Elsie said, "Oh – now! Eighth or ninth mebbe."

Bonfield waved the letter. "It's her ladyship. Comin' on the eleventh. Best bibs and tuckers will be worn." He paused and thought for a moment. "It's maybe the will has brought her scurrying down from Perthshire – at last!"

Elsie was more interested in the two pounds than her ladyship's letter. "Where'd ye get it?" she asked, and when he looked blank added, "The money."

"My pay, Elsie," said Bonfield, the patient man. "Only my entitlement as a soldier awaiting honourable discharge from His Majesty's Service."

Elsie did not seem impressed. Bonfield embraced and kissed her, and at the same time – he was very adept at this kind of thing – managed to extract a key from her apron pocket. It was for the cupboard where the whisky was kept.

"Oh, to damn wi' ye," cried Elsie. "I don't like this. You gallivantin' like the Laird of Cockpen – bringing David here, bringing me here, living in this place as if you owned it."

"Davie does," said Bonfield more seriously, then added, "Well, very nearly."

"Does he?" demanded Elsie, "And all this – officer's pay and ration coupons and I don't know what you're up to."

Jack Bonfield did not answer. He made his way purposefully to the cupboard, got the whisky bottle out and was pouring out a good-sized dram when Elsie took the bottle from him.

"Will you stop and listen to me?" she demanded. "A' you think about's drink . . . It's not right, is it?"

Bonfield took a swig at his dram. "I don't blame you girning," he said benevolently. "You're a kept woman, acting unpaid, but I'll keep my word. I'll marry you."

"Not while ye carry on like this, you'll not."

Bonfield changed his tune. "That boy will inherit this house," he tried to sound impressive, "and a third of the Murray-McNeil estate. You'll see."

"If it wasn't for the sake of that boy," said Elsie angrily, "I wouldnae wait to see anything."

That boy was at the moment outside the door, listening to everything they said. Over his brief years he had never stopped worrying about his future, so he took every opportunity to listen to his elders' conversation. Now he heard Bonfield say, "Wilkie the lawyer assured me if Sir Archie made a soldier's will in the field – and he did, for I saw him do it – it will be legal."

"Why's it takin' so long, then?"

"I don't know," admitted Bonfield. "I'm a manservant – no' a fortune teller."

Elsie shook her head. "But in the meantime you'll dress up in the uniform of a master killed for King and Country and carry on deceits and lies and I don't know a' what."

"I'm doing my best to make ends meet," protested Bonfield.

"You'll get us a' the jail."

Bonfield shook his head and Elsie shouted, "You get the jail for yourself, for you're no' gettin' it for me."

"What else can I do?" pleaded Bonfield. "The lawyer and the banker can't dole out funds on my say-so and I cannae ask her ladyship to keep his son by another woman." Elsie looked puzzled. "He never told her," explained Bonfield. "How could he? They'd gone their own ways years back."

It was Elsie's turn to shake her head. Bonfield looked down at his dram, then raised his head and looked her straight in the eyes. "I know what you think," he said, "but I've only done what the master bid me. Found David in that Godforsaken institute in Falkirk where they'd put him after his mother died, brought you to look after him here, and – illegitimate or no' – until that boy gets his rights I'll not give up. I've my duty to do and by God I will do it."

Elsie relented. "I don't know why," she said. "I cannae trust you, but I will." She paused, then added, "I'm sorry."

"Say no more." Bonfield handed over his Sam Browne belt and his uniform jacket, then suddenly took the jacket back and picked out a packet of cigarettes from a side pocket. When he thought Elsie wasn't looking, he extracted the documents from the breast pocket. She was going out with the uniform. "Hang them out of harm's way in the lobby press," he said. "Oh, take the ration books, Elsie, and do your best. A wee celebration – we're winning the war at last."

Outside the door David judged that his eavesdropping should be over. He went upstairs to his bed before Elsie could discover him.

He took a book into bed with him. It was the poems of Robert Burns. He lay there puzzling out language that he felt he should know but didn't. There was a tap at the door and Bonfield, his hero, came in with a glass of whisky in his hand. "Lights out, Davie," he said. "Ten o'clock, when decent folk should a' be sleepin' sound." He looked at the book in Davie's hands. "You fond of Burns, Davie?" he asked.

"I don't understand all the words," replied David. "I like poetry, though."

"Do you?" said Bonfield. He was expansive. "Well, I'm not averse to a well-turned rhyme. They all go on about Rabbie, but I prefer Sir Walter . . . Scott, you know."

"No, I don't know him."

"My favourite," Bonfield was beaming now. "And your father's, incidentally." He squared his shoulders and quoted –

"Oh! would it had been so! –
not then my poor heart

Had learned the sad lesson,
to love and to part;
To bear unassisted its burden of care,
While I toiled for the wealth,
I had no one to share."

David looked impressed, as he really did at anything Bonfield said. But Bonfield, whisky taken, was in another world. "Great man," he said, going back to Scott. "There's none of 'A man's a man for a' that' about him. Sir Walter was a gentleman – not a radical bone in his body. Still Scottish, but a gentleman."

He swallowed the last of his dram. "Same as your father was," he told David. "A man might well be a man, Davie, but a gentleman's a gentleman. Don't you forget it. You're a Murray-McNeil. Lairds of the Strath of Donald since Adam was a boy." He turned the gas down to a peep.

David peered at him through the gloom. "Why would he not marry my mother?" he asked. Bonfield said easily, "Cause he was married already and she wouldn't divorce him. It's not been easy for you, Davie, I know that."

"It wasnae right," objected David.

Bonfield paused. "Davie," he said, "there are rules and sometimes the very best people break the rules. It's no' right. You're right there, but sometimes it takes courage to do it."

"He never came to see me," objected David. "For years now, he never came back."

"He sent money, Davie," said Bonfield reasonably. "He felt he'd been unfair to your mother – that she might've married somebody else if he hadn't – and he'd a position to keep up too."

"He should've come," said David stubbornly. "Why did he not?"

"I've told you," said Bonfield patiently. "Before he died – the night before – he had a premonition, I suppose you would call it. He asked me to find you and bring you up – told me he was sorry – told me he'd left this place and money for you to make it up."

"He was ashamed o' us," said David bitterly.

"No, David, no," Bonfield was urgent. "I knew your father from when he was a boy. I served him through his life – through right and wrong. I went to war wi' him even though I didnae have to, just because I thought he was the finest man I ever knew in a' my life. He lived true to his own lights. 'Semper Fidelis' – 'Always Faithful.' Maybe he made mistakes – God knows we all do – but he was a shining, lovely man, full of kindness and concern. It was an honour to serve him, and I promise you this – I'm your man as I was your father's. I'll bring you up here as he asked me. All right?"

"Aye," said David, then swallowed. "How did my father die . . . was he shot?"

"Shell, Davie," answered Bonfield. "It was a stray mortar shell. Early morning patrol, hissel' and me." He looked back on the day. "We buried what we could," he said. "Life's not without its problems, but we must just soldier on, David. It's a long way to Tipperary."

Bonfield went to the bedroom door, then turned and took the signet ring off his finger. He handed it to David, saying, "It was your father's signet. It'll be too big for you, but it's a talisman, ye might say, to let you know who it is you are."

David examined the ring. He saw the motto, "Semper Fidelis," which meant nothing to him. He looked up at Bonfield with questioning eyes, but his hero was waving good-night.

* * *

Jack Bonfield, Elsie thought, was at it again. He was standing in front of the wardrobe mirror admiring himself in a Black Watch mess jacket.

"Ye're gettin' gey fond o' dressing up in the uniforms, are ye no'?" she said.

"Oh," said Bonfield, "just giving them an airing." He looked complacently at his reflection. "I'd've made a good officer, mind you."

Elsie didn't know what to say. But, sure enough, after their high tea in the evening, Bonfield was there in the full Black Watch officer's mess dress, urging David to learn the steps of the eightsome reel. He kept shouting out instructions, but David didn't seem to follow.

"It's no' easy for the boy," complained Elsie. "An eightsome reel wi' only his own partner to learn it."

"It's easy enough," stated Bonfield. "Never make a Highland officer and gentleman this way."

"Havers!" said Elsie. "Find a waltz among the records."

Bonfield did as he was told, and in a moment Elsie was waltzing with David. The boy, with his eyes closed, was dancing well. "Spitting image of the master," said Bonfield.

The doorbell clanged. "Eight o'clock on a Sunday night?" said Bonfield, puzzled. He nodded to Elsie to answer the door. Outside a calm but strong voice asked, "Is there a Captain Semple lives here?"

"No, I think you've made a mistake," Bonfield heard Elsie say. "There's no one of that name here. Just a minute."

Bonfield unbuttoned his mess jacket and disappeared. When he emerged again he was wearing a butler's outfit. "What is it, Elsie?" he asked. "Who is it?"

The man in the doorway said, "We're looking for a Captain Semple. You're not him, sir?"

"Me? No," said Bonfield. "I'm afraid you've made a mistake."

"Who are you, sir?" asked the man.

"Who are you?" responded Bonfield boldly.

"Irvine," said the man quietly. "Sergeant Irvine, Glasgow C.I.D. This is Constable Boreland." He indicated his colleague just behind him.

"I'm the butler," explained Bonfield. "At present caretaker and general factotum till the cessation of hostilities."

"Who lives here then?" asked Irvine.

"This," said Bonfield smoothly, "is the residence of the late Captain Sir Archibald Murray-McNeil, 1st Battalion, Black Watch."

"The late Captain?" echoed Irvine.

"Killed in action."

Irvine nodded his head. "Bad luck," he said. "Still, soon be over now. You can't help then?"

Bonfield shook his head and Irvine and Boreland went out into the Terrace. Bonfield couldn't help himself. He went immediately into the drawing room and watched the two detectives through the window. They were well away and that was fine. What he didn't realise was that the suspicious Sergeant Irvine had looked back at the house and had seen the movement of the curtain. Bonfield picked out the hidden paybook and tried to conceal it as Elsie came in.

She looked at him accusingly. "Is that what you're up to?" she asked. "Pretending you're . . ." Bonfield nodded towards David, and shook his head.

"You'll get us all the jail," said Elsie. "What've you been doing?"

"Nothing," said Bonfield blandly. "Make us another cup of tea, will you? Or better still, pour us a half." He went downstairs to the kitchen and thrust the incriminating paybook into the stove. Elsie saw that something was wrong.

"If you don't tell me the truth," she said, "I'm leaving

in the morning. I've never done anything dishonest in my life and I'm not going to start now."

"Elsie, will you for Heaven's sake shut up and stop nagging me. What I have done had to be done."

"What about this Captain Semple?" she kept on.

Bonfield had a peculiar look on his face. "Captain Semple," he said, "is with his Maker. Blown to bits on Flanders' Field." Elsie bowed her head. "I'm sorry," Bonfield said, "I know you're feart. If I've done anything amiss, it wasn't for gain. And there's no evidence now."

Elsie didn't know what to say. She saw young David off to bed and then went to bed herself. She was still awake when Bonfield entered with the careful tread of the man who is slightly drunk.

"I'm awake," she told him. "You in the huff?" he asked her as he started to undress.

"Is Davie all right?" asked Elsie. "His light's out anyway," consoled Bonfield. "Thinks the world of you," he added.

He got into bed and they tried to sleep. But Jack Bonfield couldn't sleep. He had to tell Elsie the true story of Captain Sir Archibald Murray-McNeil. "He killed his own men," said Bonfield brokenly. "I filled him wi' whisky for days, but it wasnae enough. A slip o' the tongue, it could only've been. He'd called a bombardment – artillery, you know – two hundred yards short of where it should've been, this side a ridge where B Platoon was bunched for a final assault. Bang in among them. Seven of them blawn to hell first go, and when Jerry got wind, a wheen of them more."

Bonfield took a deep breath. "I'd hear him groanin' in the night like a soul bereft," he went on, "banging his head on the dug-out wall. Well, he made the will and then that night, about three in the morning, I woke wi' the bang. I knew what it was and I ran. He'd blawn a hole in the side o' his heid."

He paused again and Elsie tried to prevent herself from crying out. There were tears on her face as Jack said, "I didnae want them thinkin' his nerve had cracked. I didnae want it said of a Murray-McNeil. Well, I got his jacket, put it on him, Sam Browne and helmet an' a'. I warned the sentries we were going out on a two-man recce and in the dark I lugged him away up a left flank trench, manoeuvred him over the top where the bags were loose, and out to our first wire. I waited till the dawn came up and then I propped him ready. I'd stuck a grenade in his belt and I pulled the pin and heaved him quick on to the barbed wire. He hung there with his arms spread like a crucifix. The Jerries opened up at the janglin' o' the wire and he was blawn to bits."

Elsie broke down, sobbing, and then clutched him to her breast.

* * *

It was the morning of the eleventh of November, 1918, a date which those who lived then will never forget. Bonfield, after a night of drinking and confession, lay like a log. It was all he could do to respond to young David's call. "What is it?" he asked in confusion.

"Your tea, sir," said David, proferring the cup. The boy couldn't contain himself. "The war's finished," he shouted.

Bonfield still hadn't surfaced. He could see the boy and the cup of tea, but he didn't get the message. "It's in the paper," David was still shouting. "It's the war – it's finished. The Germans have surrendered. There's to be an armistice this morning – to be signed at eleven."

Bonfield registered that a band was playing somewhere. "What the hell's a' that racket?" he demanded. "What are they playing for?"

"For the peace," David tried to get through to him. "Everybody's going daft. Everybody."

But Bonfield, instead of hailing the wonderful news, looked thoughtful and said, "This is the day her ladyship's due. It's your father's wife comin'." He looked at David. "Tell Elsie I'll be down," he said. "To put the kettle on for a shave."

Outside the people were hanging out flags, the church bells were ringing and sirens were blowing from the multitude of ships on the Clyde. But, as Bonfield went down to breakfast, the Armistice was not so much on his mind as the imminent confrontation. Elsie realised that his first concern was the meeting with Lady Murray-McNeil. "Do you really think it's the Will?" she asked.

"Not before time if it is," said Bonfield, attacking his bacon and eggs. "We'll have to look slippy," urged Elsie. "The drawing room's a disgrace."

Bonfield had started to read the morning paper. "God almighty!" he ejaculated. "Just listed to this." He read from the open page, "Lady Murray-McNeil to stand for Parliament. Labour candidate. The late Sir Archibald Murray-McNeil's widow, Lady Margaret Murray-McNeil, has been accepted by the Labour Party as a candidate for Perthshire at the first election to be held after the war. During the war she was prominent among Scottish suffragettes and rejoiced at their victory when the Votes for Women's Bill was passed through Parliament last year. While not likely to be elected in what is a safe Liberal seat, she said yesterday, 'I intend to try. Women must make sure that we win the peace after the war'." He threw the paper down. "That's what we've fought the war for," he said.

"What's wrong with it?" asked Elsie.

Bonfield frowned. "The stupid bitch is standing for Parliament – as a Socialist, a Bolshevik."

The front door bell rang and they looked at each other in concern. But it was just David with Bonfield's cigarettes. He was sparkling with excitement. "Everybody's talking in the streets," he shouted. "Hanging flags out of the windows. Drunk men – lassies singing. They're off their heads, the whole lot of them."

"It's true enough, then," said Bonfield. It's actually happening?" After what he had been through, he couldn't believe that the war had come to an end.

Suddenly on the air came the sound of church bells in the distance, then a ship's siren from the Clyde and a factory whistle. "It's the bells!" David couldn't stop shouting. "They'd to be rung at eleven."

Bonfield led the way upstairs to the front door, followed by Elsie and David. They stood on the steps and listened to the sounds of victory. They waved to the happy people who waved to them. Elsie wept.

David looked at her with concern. Why should anybody cry when the war was over? Suddenly he remembered that this was the day when the great lady was coming. He turned, alarmed, to Bonfield. "She's not going to take me away, is she? Her that's coming?"

"No, Davie," said Bonfield firmly. "Nobody's going to take you away. All right?"

He led the way back into the house. And just then, up the hill in Kelvingrove, came Sergeant Irvine and Constable Boreland of the C.I.D. They had reached the statue of Lord Roberts, now festooned with somebody's decoration of little red, white and blue flags, when Boreland said, "Will you lift him?"

"If it's him," returned Irvine.

"But how do you know?"

Sergeant Irvine was always patient. "Oh, I've no proof," he said, "no' without facing him with the bank clerk. I'd want a bit more before I took him down to the station to do that." He brought out a pocket book and took some Army official papers from it, showing the papers to Boreland. "It's an honourable discharge and something else," he said, "a mention in dispatches."

Boreland was amazed, "That right? A hero, eh?"

"I only noticed it second time of reading," said the Sergeant. "Maybe he's done a bit and hasnae got a pension – wife and weans to keep, nae doubt."

"Livin' up there?" Boreland was incredulous as he looked up at the House on the Hill. "You're gettin' soft."

Irvine gave a wry smile. "It's you that's the Socialist, you're the John MacLean, the Keir Hardie man. Concern for the underdog." He paused and shrugged. "Seems funny too, liftin' a hero on Armistice Day. Come on, soon be dark."

* * *

They were back in the kitchen. David was waiting apprehensively for the arrival of the lady. Elsie was ironing an apron. Bonfield, in his shirt sleeves, was still reading the newspaper as if he couldn't believe it. The door bell jangled. "That's her!" cried Bonfield. "Damn – my coat."

"What do I call her?" asked Elsie. "Is it 'your Ladyship'?"

"That'll do fine," said Bonfield, as they reached the ground floor landing. "Don't open the door to her till I'm up the stairs."

He darted up the stairs. Elsie took a deep breath, then opened the door. There was Lady Murray-McNeil, not quite as intimidating as Elsie anticipated.

"Oh," said the Lady, "I expected Bonfield. May I come in?"

She didn't wait for an answer but walked directly into the hall. She looked at Elsie with interest and asked, "You're . . ?"

"Elsie, your ladyship. I'm the housekeeper. Mr. Bonfield won't be a moment." And at that moment Bonfield came hurrying down the stairs, the complete butler. "My lady," he bowed. "Do come in, ma'am," and ushered Lady Murray-McNeil into the drawing room. He lit the fire and turned to her. "May I say how good it is to see you, ma'am? You look well despite the rigours."

"Of age, Bonfield?"

"Oh – the war I was going to say, ma'am."

She looked round her. "Goodness," she confessed. "I'd forgotten this place. It's nicer than I remembered." She wandered round the room, looking at pictures and photographs and stopped at one of Sir Archie in Black Watch uniform. She clasped her hands to her eyes. Bonfield was concerned, "Elsie's making tea, ma'am. Would you rather be alone for a bit?"

"No, no, Bonfield," Lady Murray-McNeil took her hands from her eyes. "I've come to talk, after all." She sat at the window, looking out at the twilight descending on the park. "I've been to see the lawyer," she went on. "This isn't easy. I'm speaking mistress to servant, but it's past that now. I've had a shock. I knew there had been another woman, but until Mr. Wilkie broke it to me today, I didn't know there had been – there *is* a son. What a fool I must have seemed. And you've been burdened with secrets that must have made you feel disloyal."

"I cannae say they did, ma'am."

Lady Murray-McNeil turned her head from the window and looked at him.

"You were my husband's man – I understood that – but I can't help feeling betrayed. Why don't you speak? It was you who first coaxed my middle-class ignorance into some kind of ladyship. I thought there might still be some echo of that time. Never mind – at least you're consistent. Light the light."

Bonfield held a taper to the fire and lit the gas lamp. He turned to the lady and cleared his throat. "I've been a good servant," he said. "But I had to choose – harder for me than anyone knew – between the family and the man. I chose the man."

"Servants and masters!" exclaimed Lady Murray-McNeil. "Well, we'll change all that now it's over."

"With deference, my lady, you'll never do that."

"They said we'd never get the vote. And we'll get into Parliament too. The system has to be changed – not only for women, for everyone. 'The people's flag' has been dyed too long in blood, shed in capitalist wars and capitalist sweat-shops."

Bonfield was indignant. "You're betraying your class," he said.

"Not mine. His class. Your class. What faith are you keeping? Even in his grave, you're keeping Archie's lack of it alive. There's only one duty, Bonfield. To be who you are."

For the first time Bonfield looked at her as a man, not a servant. "You are what you're given. I was given Bonfield by a suitable young footman who was wedded wi' my mother three months gone and absconded with the old Laird's dowry when he'd given me his name."

"I never knew," said Lady Murray-McNeil, a whit dismayed.

"It was never said except in gossip. But it's that that's driven me a' my days – to be some man's son. So don't you ask me who I am. And don't you deceive me wi' Bolshevik jargon. The people's blood! What blood? There's nae blood in you. The martyred dead would turn in their shrouds to see you beneath their banner." He paused, then added, "I've kept my faith, and if you'd done the same . . ."

"You think *he* did? Where was faith? With women in

Glasgow? In nights, week-ends, in years of not coming home? He never forgave that I wouldn't divorce him. This boy was his heir. He wanted his name – the title – to go on. It makes me sick – absent lairds and waiting ladies, English accents in kilts, betraying the people's dignity, piping them to death on foreign fields and blethering like you about duty and faith. And in the end he's betrayed you and betrayed his son as your father did you. There's no will made with mention of a son and nothing left for you forbye a pittance."

"That's the old will," said Bonfield triumphantly.

"There isn't any other. I spent the morning with my lawyer. The army can trace no will made by him in the trenches."

Bonfield played his trump card. "I saw Sir Archie write it – the day before he died. The Adjutant was witness and another officer. He put it in an envelope and sealed it with wax. Then he put it, methodical like, in his breast pocket. And that very next morning . . ." He stopped suddenly, thinking of Sir Archie on the barbed wire. "Oh, God Almighty! I see what I've done."

"I don't understand," said Lady Murray-McNeil.

"There is no will. There's no inheritance for the boy and it's me that's to blame. What it was, when Sir Archie died, that will was on him and he was – there was – I'm sorry to distress ye –"

He could not go on. Sir Archie's widow said levelly, "There was nothing left to bury, is that it?" Bonfield nodded miserably.

"Were you with him?" she asked, more gently. Bonfield nodded again.

The front-door bell rang. "I'll see to that," said Bonfield and went into the hall. On the doorstep were the two detectives. "It's us again, sir," said the Sergeant. "Sorry to bother you, but it just occurred to me that –"

"I've a very important visitor with me at the moment. It can't wait, can it?"

"Won't take a tick, sir," Irvine said and walked into the hall, followed by Constable Boreland. Bonfield felt he was trapped. "You better just step in here," he said and ushered them into the dining room.

Sergeant Irvine came straight to the point. He held up a wallet. "Would this be yours, sir?" Bonfield nodded. Once again he seemed incapable of speech. "You hadn't missed it? Over the week-end?"

"Yes," Bonfield managed to utter.

"We have our uses," confided Irvine. "We were passing and it occurred to me that if Captain Semple didn't live here, maybe Lance Corporal Bonfield did. I took the liberty," he opened the wallet and took out the papers, "and there was your honourable discharge inside. See, this Captain Semple has been signing cheques against his army pay for quite a time now. He had all the relevant papers – identity, pay record, account number. But last week he left your – I mean, his pocket book on the counter. Well, the clerk opened it, saw these – your papers – and was suspicious. The manager checked with the Black Watch depot. The real Captain Semple – killed in action last March."

Bonfield tried to collect himself. He had heard a sound outside the door and wondered if it was David, whose bad habit it was to listen at doors. And what was happening about Lady Murray-McNeil?

"Well, there you are," he said lamely. "This fellow must have –"

"Picked your pocket?" suggested Irvine. "Of course, there is another possibility. Supposing the pocket book wasn't stolen. Supposing the uniform, identity, pay-record had been . . . acquired?"

* * *

David had been listening at the door. He was worried about his hero, Bonfield. What did these men want with him? He was dithering about in the hall when Elsie appeared from downstairs. "Ah, there you are," she said, and took him by the hand. "We'll go into the drawing room 'cause you should meet Lady Murray-McNeil."

It was the last thing David wanted to do, but he couldn't get away. In they went and there was this lady standing in front of the fireplace with a cup of tea in her hand. Elsie gave him a little push forward. "This is David, my lady," she said.

Lady Murray-McNeil's eyes widened as she looked at David. She thought of an old phrase of her childhood – he's the spitting image of Archie. Her heart gave an accustomed turn.

"We've maybe intruded," said Elsie and took David by the shoulder to indicate they should go. "No, no, please don't," cried the lady. "I'm perfectly well." She looked at David more closely. "Well, you're a surprise."

Elsie introduced him, but David didn't know what to say. Lady Murray-McNeil seemed to have collected herself. "My goodness," she said, "you're like – your father."

"I'll get some hot water," broke in Elsie. "Freshen up the tea."

David seemed to realise the lady was not a dragon after all. "They're lighting a bonfire in the park," he said.

"A bonfire?" echoed Lady Murray-McNeil.

"For the end of the war," explained David, in the indulgent way that children speak to adults who don't know the answers.

"We'll ask Mr. Bonfield," said Elsie and out she went.

There was an awkward pause and then the lady said, "Have a cake." "No, thanks," said David. "Or a sandwich?" David refused again.

"I won't eat you, you know," said Lady Murray-

McNeil. David lifted his head and looked at her. She smiled and he smiled back. The lady's look lingered and then she turned back to the window which looked out on the park. She was thinking, in spite of everything, how she had loved Archie. Had it been her fault that the marriage ended in failure? This boy was what might have been. She turned and looked at David again.

"Are you happy, David? Are you all right here?"

David said yes.

"You like it with Elsie and Mr. Bonfield?"

David said yes again.

"Good," said Lady Murray-McNeil, suddenly making up her mind. "Then that'll be all right. I'll see to it – I'll see you have everything your father would have wanted you to have."

David didn't quite understand what she was saying to him. "Can I go to the bonfire?" he asked.

"Of course," smiled Lady Murray-McNeil. "Can I come too?" She picked up her coat as David walked across the hall to the dining room. He opened the door just as one of the two men he didn't like was saying, "So you see, sir, that's how I think it really was. What do *you* think?"

David couldn't be bothered with grown-up conversation. "They're lighting the bonfire in the park at seven," he said to Bonfield. "Are you not finished?"

"Aye, aye, Davie," Bonfield said hastily. "Now don't interrupt."

"The lady's coming too."

"You go with her and Elsie," instructed Bonfield. "I'll be down at your back."

As David left the room Sergeant Irvine said, sympathetically for him, "Would you like to tell me about it, sir?"

Bonfield cleared his throat, but his voice was still thick when he spoke. "Semple – Captain Semple – was killed at

Poelcapple. Three weeks after Sir Archie. I was bound for Blighty. They gave me his papers to take back to Regimental H.Q. In all the excitement, I forgot – not intentionally, though. It was only after we were in this house that I came across them. It occurred to me, with most of the bank clerks that would have known him at the war themselves, I might get away with drawing his pay for a month or two." He paused, then said with some dignity, "It wasn't for myself, you understand. It was for the boy till he got his inheritance."

"Would you go with Constable Boreland and get your coat?"

"What happens now?" asked Bonfield.

"I'll have to take you down to the station."

"What'll I get?"

Detective-Sergeant Irvine's face almost softened. "I'll do my best for you," he said. "Now go on."

Bonfield, accompanied by Constable Boreland, walked up the stairs just as Elsie came up from the kitchen. "What is it?" she asked Irvine.

"I'm sorry," he answered. "Your husband is –"

"He's no' my husband, but – you're taking him?"

"I've got to," Irvine explained. "No, no, missis, don't worry. I'm sure they'll be lenient."

"What's he done?" asked Elsie fearfully.

"Impersonating an officer, defrauding the bank, forging cheques. You cannae do these things, even them that's done their bit."

Bonfield came downstairs with the detective-constable. He looked at her and said, "Elsie, I'm sorry."

"Oh, Jack!" the tears were brimming in her eyes.

"Don't worry," he said, with a touch of his old bravado. "I'll be back."

Boreland snapped the handcuffs on his wrists and, just as they moved to the front door, the bell jangled and they could see David's face pressed against the decorated glass.

Irvine opened the door and David shouted, "Come on, come on. They're going to start. I came back for you."

"Davie," said Bonfield brokenly. He lifted his hand to pat David's head and the boy saw that he was handcuffed. He screamed, and Elsie took David into her arms. The boy broke away from her and ran after Bonfield, beating at Boreland and then trying to catch Bonfield's coat. "Let him go! Let him go!" he screamed. "Mr. Bonfield – Mr. Bonfield!"

Detective-Sergeant Irvine took David firmly by the shoulders and turned him back to Elsie. Boreland and Bonfield hurried away into the darkness. There was a great roar as the bonfire suddenly went up in the park. David didn't see the bonfire. He had broken down completely and was howling with a great sense of loss.

Up the steps came Lady Murray-McNeil. She had seen enough to know full well what had happened. She looked with infinite compassion on David sobbing, back in Elsie's arms. And she decided what she must do.

# EPILOGUE

The sun was shining in the windows of the House on the Hill. It was the summer of 1931 and the glancing rays fell on David, now twenty-five, and looking more like his father than ever, and on his fiancée, Grace. They also fell on the signet ring which Bonfield had given him all these years ago – his father's ring with the family motto, "Semper Fidelis". The couple were looking at some old photographs.

"That's Elsie," pointed out David.

"I thought she'd be older from all you've told me," said Grace. "She must have been like a mother to you."

"A bit more," said David reflectively. "That picture

was taken just at the end of the war – and that's Bonfield's shadow while he was taking the photograph."

"Have you a photograph of Bonfield?"

David picked out another picture. "How handsome," cried Grace, as she looked at the man wearing the uniform of a Captain in the Black Watch, topped by a jaunty Glengarry bonnet.

"What happened to Bonfield?"

"Got two years for his – trouble," said David. "He came back to us – by this time my mother had taken Elsie and me to Blairdonald. You see, she fulfilled all that Bonfield had told her my father had written in the will that was destroyed. So the house and a third of the estate became mine. She wanted to put things right. She adopted me and brought me up."

"But she didn't get into Parliament?"

David laughed. "Oh, no – but she's threatening to join the Scottish Nationalists."

"She won't have much time for an English daughter-in-law, then," smiled Grace. "And is Bonfield still with her?"

David shook his head. "With my father gone, he couldn't adapt, couldn't forgive himself. Broke Elsie's heart – but he went away in spite of her. He's out there somewhere – roving the world, building the Empire, and drinking whisky in Caledonian clubs to ease his guilt. I wish he wasn't. I wish he was home and safe."

From the window they saw Lady Murray-McNeil and Elsie arrive and hurried to open the door. "Mother," said David and they embraced. "And this is Grace – my mother." They murmured greetings.

"And this is Elsie," said David proudly. He told them, "I've just been showing Grace the house – reviving memories."

They went into the drawing room and Elsie paused at

the door. "I'll make some tea," she announced, closed the door and went back into the hall. As she walked towards the stairs which led down to the kitchen she hovered for a moment at the hallstand. There it was, still in the place where Bonfield had left it – Sir Archie's Glengarry. What was that family motto that Bonfield was always talking about? She could never remember the Latin. But she did remember the translation – "Always Faithful".

# 1934 CREDITS and DISTINCTIONS

# Credits and Distinctions · 1934

The Depression had arrived in Britain from the United States of America. In the early Thirties people had grown accustomed to the popular song, "Buddy, Can You Spare a Dime?" They had read about New York stockbrokers diving to death from skyscraper office windows. The Depression in Britain was not so dramatic, but it was deeply felt. The unemployed marchers filled the roads going to demonstrations in London. Prices were rising and wages were falling. The play that everybody talked about was called "Love on the Dole".

But in Glasgow Maisie Gifford quietly congratulated herself that she was all right. She was a dressmaker. She had come up the hard way, scorned at school, having an illegitimate daughter when she was too young to realise the dangers which could beset her, working long and hard hours in factories which should not have been allowed to exist, trying to better herself against what had at first seemed fearful odds.

And now she had made it. Her wealthy West End clientele called her a modiste. She knew she was still a dressmaker – but a very good dressmaker. She had made enough money to buy this House on the Hill. She had turned the dining room into a fitting room and just across the hall was the drawing room in which she gave tea to influential clients. She even had a maid called Alice, who wore a uniform, looked nice and spoke properly. Elsewhere in the house were rooms where her small staff could work. And that still left plenty of space for her daughter Cora and herself. She reflected, as she looked out of the fitting room, with its background of dressmakers' dummies and its swatches of material that she was much better off in this year of 1934 than most of the people she had known in the East End.

She was thinking of the East End as she looked out of the window on to Park Terrace. The vista over Kelvingrove Park did not particularly attract her, though she knew it was a good talking point for customers – tut, tut – she meant clients.

Maisie was small, neat, good looking and almost alarmingly immaculate. Her black dress was offset by a gleaming white collar and cuffs. And she was frowning because she was expecting rich clients and the scene in Park Terrace did not please her at all. First of all there was that terrible band of four or five men, playing what they intended to be the latest pantomime songs, and led by a down-at-heel character carrying an outstretched battered hat for contributions and wearing a placard round his neck. It read in ill-written letters, "Unemployed – Families to Support".

That was bad enough, but they were marching out of sight. What worried her much more was that the rag-and-bone man's cart had arrived. He had disappeared into her basement to collect a bundle of cloth scraps, and his incredibly dirty daughter was sitting in the driver's place, holding the horse's reins. Maisie shuddered. What if Mrs. Ramsay saw the cart and its occupants? Mrs. Ramsay was "Kelvinsaide" and really a very stupid woman, but she knew everybody in the West End and was recommending her "modiste" to her friends. The trouble was, thought Maisie in rather more human vein, that the wee girl would look quite pretty if she was cleaned up and properly dressed.

She jumped as Cora's voice behind her said, "I said I'm away, mother." She turned and looked at Cora – sixteen and, although Maisie said it herself, almost beautiful. And she looked so well in the uniform of the swanky school that Maisie had sent her to. But it would never do to let her know that.

"Have you brushed your teeth?" she demanded.

"Yes, I've brushed my teeth," said Cora, with a big smile to prove it was true. "Why else have I to come home for my lunch?"

"You've to come home for your lunch so I can see what you're eating." Maisie walked to the girl, straightened her tie and brushed some imaginary dust from her shoulder.

"You could see a packed lunch," said Cora. She loved to irritate her mother. She was fond of irritating people.

"You need something hot in the middle of the day."

"The other girls manage," said Cora patiently. "And they've half an hour's netball as well."

"I don't care."

"Not even if I'm a misfit?" complained Cora.

"You?" Maisie was incredulous. "I thought you said you were outrageously popular."

Cora laughed. "Only because I'm a fatherless waif with a possessive mother." She shrugged her shoulders. "It'll wear off."

A car horn sounded from the street and Maisie hurried back to the window. It couldn't have been worse. The scrap man had just emerged from the basement with his big bundle and his daughter was bending double to stow the stuff away. A big car, driven by a chauffeur, was manoeuvring round the cart. Two ladies were sitting in it, peering out to see what the trouble was.

"Mrs. Ramsay!" cried Maisie. "She's brought her upper-crust friend with her, and there's the scrap-man's wee girl climbing about, showing all she's got. What a sight!"

Cora laughed. "Will I give her a penny?"

Maisie nodded. "And say if they want the scraps from the workroom, they'll need to come early, before clients start arriving."

Cora waved and went out. Maisie turned towards the stairs, calling for Alice. She was already going up the stairs when the maid appeared. "Mrs. Ramsay and Mrs. Milne for the fitting room," she ordered. "Say I'll be down when I've washed my hands. Tea in the drawing room later, and remember the lump sugar this time."

Alice bowed her head cheerfully. She was thinking that never before had she had a mistress who spent so much time washing her hands. She went to the front door to welcome the important clients in a respectful manner.

* * *

Maisie Gifford was on her knees, pinning the ineffable Mrs. Ramsay into a new dress. Mrs. Milne, whom Maisie had disliked on sight, sat in an armchair in a negligent manner, indicating that she was bored with Mrs. Ramsay and the whole affair.

But Mrs. Ramsay never noticed nuances like that. She knew she was wonderful. As she looked around the fitting room, she said, "You've got this looking awfully nice now, Mrs. Gifford. Quite tasteful, really."

Maisie didn't even look up. "I'm pleased with it," she said flatly.

"I should think you are." Mrs. Ramsay turned to the drooping Mrs. Milne. "Bit of a difference from Barkhill Road, is it not, Florence?" She condescended to Maisie once again. "You made me the little blue crepe-de-Chine with the sweetheart neckline in Barkhill Road. Third flat – you can't imagine what some people did on the stair!"

"I've been lucky," said Maisie and rose to her feet.

Mrs. Ramsay moved over to the full-length mirror. She positively cooed. "Oh, I think so. Don't you, Florence? I really think so?"

"Are you standing quite straight?" asked Mrs. Milne languidly.

"Of course I am," replied Mrs. Ramsay with a touch of indignation.

"I'm just thinking," said Mrs. Milne in her superior way. "The pin tucks on the bodice. Does anyone wear pin tucks these days? Are they not a wee bit passé?"

Mrs. Ramsay looked worried, but Maisie went to a table and lifted a magazine. "Not according to this, Mrs. Milne," she said. "Though, of course, you'd be the better judge."

"And what's this?" asked Mrs. Milne in her most bored voice.

"A sketch in *Vogue*, latest edition, page 34," said Maisie shortly. "From the Paris Collections."

"Oh, hear that!" shouted Mrs. Ramsay. "When you can get it all in Glasgow, why go to Paris? Or London?" She turned to Maisie and explained, "Mrs. Milne buys her clothes in London."

"Really?" said Maisie, looking at Mrs. Milne's outfit appraisingly. "They're very elegant."

Mrs. Milne was still leafing through *Vogue*. She looked up at Maisie. "Can you do copies from sketches?"

"I have done," said Maisie, starting to help Mrs. Ramsay out of the new dress.

"Successfully?"

Maisie looked directly at her. "No one's ever complained."

Mrs. Ramsay gave what she felt was a cheerful laugh.

"I think you're gaining yourself another customer," she said.

"My order book's rather full at the moment," and Maisie again looked straight at Mrs. Milne.

Mrs. Ramsay was not a whit abashed. "Oh, but you'll make room for Mrs. Milne," she cried. "She'd be a wonderful advertisement – she's seen everywhere. Mrs. Milne launched a ship – did you know that?"

"No," said Maisie.

"It was in all the papers," said Mrs. Ramsay in a tone which indicated that anyone who hadn't read this news was probably illiterate. "I always fancied a launching myself. But the way things are going today, there'll never be another one."

Mrs. Milne was paying no attention to Mrs. Ramsay. She had stopped at a page in *Vogue* and now pointed at a sketch and said to Maisie, "Could you do this?"

Maisie looked at the drawing for a moment and said off-handedly, "It shouldn't be very difficult. But I'm really very busy."

"Oh, come on," cried Mrs. Ramsay. "We're all friends. We've daughters at the same school when all's said and done."

"Your girl's at St. Elizabeth's?" Mrs. Milne arched her eyebrows.

As Maisie nodded Mrs. Ramsay said, "Even if a girl's not clever, she still leaves St. Elizabeth's with something – a tidy mind – and a bit of class."

"Cora's clever," said Maisie. "She's very clever. You'll have some tea?" She took the ladies across to the drawing room. And, after tea, she saw them out to the big car and the chauffeur. As the car drew away from the House on the Hill Mrs. Milne said thoughtfully, "She seems competent."

"I think she's positively artistic," gushed Mrs. Ramsay. "And very reasonable. She's saved me an absolute mint!" She paused. "Are you going to talk to her about our wee scheme, Florence?"

"We'll see," answered Mrs. Milne, leaning forward and looking out of the window at a well-known figure. "Is that George Barton?"

"Yes," said Mrs. Ramsay. "George Barton, the lawyer."

The ladies looked at each other. Mrs. Milne's eyebrows went up once again, and Mrs. Ramsay nodded with meaning.

As the car went down the hill and turned into the West End Mrs. Ramsay said, "Mrs. Gifford – she's quite refined, is she not? And the daughter has lovely manners. You'd wonder how they learned – people like that."

* * *

Oh, yes, Cora was clever. But what Mrs. Ramsay called her "lovely manners" were kept strictly for social occasions. In her class at St. Elizabeth's she was principally famous for what was called "taking a rise out of the teacher" – not every teacher, of course, but certainly those who were weak or soft. The girls in Cora's class thought she was a scream. And this, naturally, increased Cora's desire to show off. She knew that she was ahead of the other girls and was always determined to prove it.

Now she had finished the work which Miss Geddes, an amiable, elderly woman who always reminded Cora of the sheep in *Alice Through the Looking Glass,* had set the class. Cora was bored and she also wanted to demonstrate that she had finished first. She looked up at Miss Geddes and then raised her hand a few inches above the surface of her desk. Miss Geddes stirred uneasily. "Yes, Cora?" she asked.

Cora looked at the teacher with blank innocence. "I'm sorry, Miss Geddes?"

"You'd a question?"

"No, Miss Geddes."

"Then why was your hand raised?"

"Because," Cora paused for effect. "I'm not sure that I want to say why, Miss Geddes."

The class had stopped working. They were nudging each other in anticipation of another performance by good old Cora.

Miss Geddes persisted. "I'd like to hear why your hand was raised."

"I'm sorry, Miss Geddes," said Cora sweetly. She looked round the class to make sure that they were all appreciating her. "But I don't understand how you can say you'd *like* to hear why before you've actually heard. You may not *like* the reason at all."

There was a giggle from the back of the class. Miss Geddes flushed and asked as nastily as she could, "Why was your hand raised?"

Cora said, "Well," then paused for effect. "I'm afraid I was admiring the delicate turn of my wrist, Miss Geddes, and the perfect pink almond shapes of my nails."

There was a burst of laughter from the class. Miss Geddes realised that their concentration was broken. She said to Cora, "Your attention should have been on your work."

"Oh, but it was," replied Cora, "until I'd finished it."

"Bring it to me."

Cora was all too ready. She took up her exercise book, held it open and marched to the front of the class, placing it down triumphantly before the teacher. "I don't think there are any mistakes," she said.

A brief glance showed Miss Geddes that the work was perfectly done. "Go back to your desk, Cora," she said. But she realised that the session had been ruined. Cora went back to her desk and immediately started talking with her nearest neighbours. The talk spread and the whole classroom was in an uproar. Miss Geddes was hopelessly flustered. She realised the girls were out of her control and all she could do was bleat, "Girls, I would like to remind you . . . This is quite intolerable . . . Will you, please . . .? Could you simply resume your seats?" There was a momentary lull and the teacher said, "Then I have no alternative but to detain some of you after school."

She named Cora and her two neighbours. They laughed uproariously. But, when the school bell rang for dismissal and the rest of the class had hurried out, Miss Geddes indicated as sternly as she could that they must stay. They sat in their seats and then they started laughing again. Miss Geddes's face was crimson, but she pulled a book from her desk and bent her head over it.

* * *

George Barton, respectable Glasgow lawyer, and Maisie Gifford, fashionable city modiste, were in bed together in the House on the Hill. Suddenly Maisie raised herself and looked at the bedside clock. "Hurry, George," she urged. "It's nearly half-past."

George got out of bed and started to put his clothes on. Maisie could see that he was irritated. "This is no life for a man like me," he stated. "Or a woman like you, Maisie."

Maisie was busy putting her own clothes on. "What do you mean, this is no life?"

"I mean," said George heavily, "sending the servant away to the shops, snatching half an hour before Cora comes in from school."

"I can't have you staying overnight. It would upset her."

George sighed wearily. "We should be married," he said. "After all, there's no obstacle."

Maisie was already at the wash-hand basin, washing her hands as usual. "I want more time," she said.

"You've had two years," protested the lawyer.

"Don't start again. You know the reasons."

"Oh, I know the reasons," said George ruefully. "I just don't think they're very good ones. Cora's growing up now. She likes me. She'll be wanting to lead her own life, with her own friends –"

"Not for a while," broke in Maisie and turned from the basin to the bed. She began to remake it briskly.

"You've proved your point about the business," George said. "You bought the house with your own money."

"I certainly did," snapped Maisie.

"Though heaven knows why you wanted it when I've a perfectly solid home of my own that we could all have lived in quite comfortably."

"I like my work."

"Listen," George urged. "I can buy and sell your business. You'd never want for anything with me."

Maisie looked at him. "I'd have to sack the women in the workroom. Their husbands are unemployed. You don't know what that's like. I do. I've relied on myself since I was thirteen. You can't imagine the squalor of those years after I left the High School. And then Cora when I was twenty-two. My little mistake." She waved her arms round the room. "That's what this is all about. Making myself decent when people told me I never would be. Making us both decent, me and Cora."

"You are decent," protested George. "You're fine. When I first saw you the night you brought that dress for my mother I thought I'd never seen anything so clean and neat. That's why I hate treating you like one of the pathetic little ten-bob tarts I used to take in the old days when I was desperate."

"Clean and neat?" repeated Maisie. "Once at school I

was made to show my dirty neck to every single girl in the class."

George tried to laugh. "I had a dirty neck at school," he said. "Always."

They kissed and went downstairs. In the hall Maisie suddenly stopped. "I'd make a bargain," she said. "If I could go on with the business, I'd marry you. If I could put my brass plate next to yours at the front door –"

"Oh, come on," objected George.

"Why not?"

"All right," said George wearily. They had had this kind of argument before. He put on his lawyer's voice. "I'll allow that there could be no moral objection to the placing of a brass plate advertising the services of a modiste or woman's dressmaker beside one announcing that herein resides a lawyer of His Majesty's calling. But there might be objections on the grounds of – well, seemliness."

"Who from?"

"You know who from," George lost his lawyer's voice. "The wives of comfortably-off Glasgow lawyers don't work. No one would like it. You'd never get any clients. You're being disingenuous, Maisie."

"I don't know what that means. Perhaps I just like things as they are." She looked at his fallen face and relented. "Come on, George – isn't it time we had a few days at the seaside again – the two of us?"

George brightened immediately. "Would you like that? What about Cora?"

"She's going on a wild flower collecting trip with the botany class for a few days at Easter."

"I'll book the hotel," said George immediately. They went into the drawing room for tea. "Cora's bound to be starving when she comes in," said Maisie.

But, by the time Alice had brought in the tea, there was

no sign of Cora. Maisie was looking worried. "She's never late," she muttered.

"It's only a few minutes," said George reasonably. "She's perhaps called in at another girl's house." He watched her as she poured the tea. "You'll have to learn not to worry so much about that girl, Maisie."

"I can't help it," Maisie confessed.

"You must try," urged George, "or you'll end up smothering her. Either that, or she'll break away and hurt you. She's full of life – she'll want her independence."

"She has all the independence she needs." Maisie walked to the window and looked out again. "What on earth's keeping her?"

She came back to the table. George did his best to keep conversation going, but Maisie's mind was fixed on Cora. At length she announced that she would 'phone the police.

"Don't be silly," said George sharply. "The police would laugh at you. It's not been half an hour yet. They've enough to do, anyway, keeping an eye on the men out of work."

"I'll send Alice to the tram stop."

Out went Alice and George Barton resumed his vain task of trying to reassure Maisie that all was well. Eventually she took up what seemed to be a permanent position at the window, and George joined her there. At last they saw the maid approaching, alone. Maisie rushed to the door, and had it open as Alice reached the foot of the steps. "There's no sign, madam," said Alice.

"Did you wait for the next tram?"

"Aye, I did. And I came away round Portland Terrace too, just to make sure. Did you try the school?"

"There's no one there," cried the agitated Maisie. She went to the telephone. "What's the name of that girl she plays chess with? Grace something? Grace what?"

Again George tried to soothe her but she looked at him

with a glare that seemed little short of hatred. She lifted the telephone, shouting, "What's her name? What's her *name*?"

And at that moment the door-bell rang. Alice ran to open the door. A policeman stood outside with a mud-stained, shaking, weeping Cora.

"My God, my God," cried Maisie. Cora threw herself into her mother's arms and sobbed.

The policeman cleared his throat. "She ran out at me up the back of Pollard Street," he explained. "It seems she's had a set-to with some bad laddie who took her purse. There's been a lot of this."

"I couldn't stop him," sobbed Cora. "I tried – I fell –"

"Did he hurt you?" asked Maisie urgently. Cora mumbled something and Maisie cried, "Did he?"

Alice was taking off her coat. "I'll away to run a bath, madam," she said briskly.

The policeman felt that justice should be done. "She doesn't seem to be badly hurt," he observed. Maisie paid no attention to him. "How did you miss the tram?" she asked Cora.

"Miss Geddes," wept Cora. "Miss Geddes kept us in the Latin class."

"Miss Geddes – the teacher?" said Maisie furiously. "How dare she? She'd no right. Come on, now. We'll get you all cleaned up." She helped Cora up the stairs. "Are you sure he didn't hurt you?" she asked.

"He," Cora could not go on.

"He what? What did he do?"

Cora moaned, "He . . . touched me! He *touched* me!"

"Oh, God," Maisie was horrified. "It's all right, wee girl. Don't cry."

* * *

"I think it's a matter now of least said, soonest mended, Mrs. Gifford." Miss Holroyd, the head mistress of St.

Elizabeth's, seemed always in complete control of the situation. "Don't you? Cora's had a terrible shock – we appreciate that, and perhaps this isn't the time to make an issue of her behaviour and its consequences." She glanced towards Miss Geddes, who hovered nearby. "We're content, Miss Geddes and I, to let it rest for the moment. I also think a week's absence is long enough, if I may say so."

Maisie faced her. She was wearing her smartest clothes, and she needed them. For Miss Holroyd's calm worried her. "I'll send her back when I think she's ready." she said, trying to control the tremor in her voice.

"Well," Miss Holroyd shook her head, "it's a certificate year, of course, and you know what that means. She's missing important work."

"She can cope with that. She's a clever girl."

"Indeed she is," agreed the headmistress. "Sometimes too clever for her own good – a little arrogant, a little inclined to distract others who do need to work hard."

Miss Geddes couldn't help herself. "You see," she said in a small voice, "that was why . . ."

She faltered as Maisie gave her a look of complete hatred.

Miss Holroyd broke in. "No girl, however bright, can afford to waste time. And the Easter holidays will be here soon."

Maisie collected herself. "You said you were content to let it rest." Miss Holroyd nodded. "Well, I'm not," said Maisie.

"I don't know what you mean," Miss Holroyd shook her head.

Maisie turned to her daughter's teacher. "Miss Geddes," she said, "you had no right to keep Cora behind after school." Miss Geddes stared at her in alarm. "I should have been given notice." Miss Geddes attempted to say something but Maisie swept on. "There's a school rule that says parents must have written notice of detention."

"I think," said the headmistress quickly, "you're confusing two separate matters here, Mrs. Gifford. Formal detention could spoil a girl's record. Miss Geddes wanted to give the girls a few minutes to control themselves and stop behaving foolishly."

"In those few minutes," said Maisie bitterly, "Cora missed her usual tram and was attacked and robbed and . . . mauled by some . . ." She could not go on.

"I know," pleaded Miss Geddes. "I can't tell you how badly I feel – what it's cost me in . . ."

Miss Holroyd rushed to the defence. "The trams are very frequent. You can't hold Miss Geddes responsible for what happened."

Maisie almost shouted. "She was on her own coming through that lane. If she'd caught the usual tram there'd have been other girls."

The headmistress stood up. "Then I suggest," she said sternly, "you impress on Cora that in future there will be no indulgence shown when she behaves foolishly. It will be formal detention, with notice." She paused and softened a little. "Perhaps her need to make her mark by showing off is to do with a relatively new girl. Why not let her bring a packed lunch and get rid of some of the energy on the netball courts? It must be difficult for you, bringing up a lively girl on your own. When did she lose her father?"

Maisie was at once furious and afraid. What did this woman know about Cora's forgotten father? "Why should you want to know anything about her father?" she demanded, and, despite her height, did her best to stalk out of the headmistress's office.

* * *

George Barton looked over the links at Largs. This holiday was a complete bore. He'd booked a double room for Maisie and himself, and now Maisie and Cora were occupying it, and he was in a single room. Not only that, but Maisie never took her eyes off Cora. He was worried too, about the forthcoming trial. The police had got the man who molested the girl. Well, that was fine, but Maisie was insisting that St. Elizabeth's and Miss Geddes in particular should be brought into it. He saw trouble ahead and was glad when they got back to Glasgow.

Maisie seemed glad too. She plunged into her work with enthusiasm. On the afternoon when she put the snooty Mrs. Milne into the dress she had created, she felt she was ready for whatever the future held. And, as she gave her two principal clients tea, Mrs. Ramsay said, "The Ladies' Circle is planning a Spring Charity Gala for next month, in aid of . . ."

Mrs. Milne came to the rescue. "Canteens for the families of the unemployed."

"Oh, is it?" said Mrs. Ramsay, taken aback. "I'm not awfully keen on that. It's just encouraging them to be idle. Well, anyway, guess what we thought up as a special attraction? A fashion show – with all the dresses made by you! We're going to model them ourselves – it's an absolute yell!"

Maisie looked doubtful. "Your name in all the papers," persuaded Mrs. Ramsay. "You'd be positively *made*!"

Maisie was slightly bemused. "There would be publicity, then?" she asked.

"Yes," said the superior Mrs. Milne. "Does that alarm you?"

"Not in the least," said Maisie, recovering herself. "There'll be another sort of publicity coming my way soon with the court case. You heard about my daughter?"

The ladies, embarrassed, indicated that they had.

"Perhaps," said Maisie bitterly, "if Miss Her Ladyship Geddes hadn't abused her authority . . ."

"Miss Geddes?" Mrs. Milne looked at Mrs. Ramsay.

"Miss Geddes is an old dear," said Mrs. Ramsay at once. "She's not strong on discipline, but she can teach."

"She's very full of herself," Maisie said. "They all are. High School teachers – they all stick together. I know – I was on a scholarship myself."

As she bade them goodbye, Maisie felt a sense that all was not well. As she waited for Cora to come home from school, she realised that all was not well with Cora either. For a whole week Cora had refused tea. She wasn't even cheeky to Maisie, who had to tell her forcibly how essential it was for them both to appear in court at the trial of "the man". It was additionally worrying that George Barton, who was acting for them in the case, was rather apprehensive about the whole outcome. Was everybody against her, Maisie asked herself. Well, she would show them. She didn't have a dirty neck now.

The trial was reported in the Glasgow newspapers in some detail. It was a change from unemployment and the Depression. There was also good stuff against the top school for girls in the city. Maisie was delighted.

There was no delight in St. Elizabeth's next morning. Miss Holroyd had called Miss Geddes in and they read a newspaper report together. It said, towards the end, "After passing sentence the Sheriff congratulated the girl on the clear and courageous way in which she gave evidence. Taking up a point from that evidence, he deplored the system whereby the girl had been detained in school without parental notice. While allowing that all young people required discipline, he felt that in the interest of safety some other arrangement should have been made."

The headmistress looked at Miss Geddes, who was crying wretchedly. She opened another newspaper which showed a picture of Maisie smiling delightedly. "Look," Miss Holroyd said, "she's pushed the unemployed off the picture page." Miss Geddes's eyes were so blurred that she couldn't see, so Miss Holroyd read out to her, "Mrs. Gifford, the fashionable modiste at present arranging the mannequin parade for the Ladies' Circle, photographed after the trial." She threw the newspaper on the floor and put her hand over the trembling hand of Miss Geddes.

"Cheer up," she said sympathetically. "She's a vulgar little person and I think she's overstepped the mark."

At that moment the "vulgar little person" was putting finishing touches to the clothes for the mannequin parade. George Barton was with her, holding a newspaper. Maisie glanced at the page briefly.

"I know," she said, oozing satisfaction. "I'd never've thought my brown barathea would have photographed so well."

George shook his head in bewilderment. "How is Cora today?" he asked.

"Quiet, but she'll bounce back. Wasn't she wonderful in the witness box?"

George looked at her thoughtfully. "Why don't you take a long rest now?"

"I will," said Maisie. "When it's all over. There's one more stage."

"And what's that?"

"In view of what was said in court, there has to be some kind of example made." George raised his eyebrows. "Of the teachers," explained Maisie patiently. "They have to be shown they can't have everything their own way. I want a prosecution, George. For neglect of duty, as the Sheriff said. I'll leave the details to you." George looked appalled, but Maisie didn't seem to notice his expression. She put her arms round him and said, "After that I'll take a long rest. I'll give up work and I'll be with you. We'll be married, George – when it's really all over."

In the embrace she couldn't see George's face, and that was just as well. Next day she had a rehearsal of the mannequin parade. A letter arrived fron George, but she didn't think it was important. It was only in one of the longeurs of the rehearsal, taken in Mrs. Milne's most superior style, that she opened it.

"My dear Maisie," she read. "I don't ever find it easy to say what I feel, as you know. But I must tell you that things are not right between us. I can't do what you ask. Even if I could, I'm convinced it would be inadvisable and might do you harm in quite unlooked-for ways. Let's take some time away from one another and consider. It will be hard for me. Much harder for you, I think – you with all your courage and independence – but necessary. Thank you, my dear, for all you've done for me. I can write no more now. Ever yours, George."

Maisie suffered the rehearsal. She didn't seem to notice that there was an undercurrent of feeling against her from the other women. All she wanted to do was to put George in his place. When she got back to the House on the Hill she wrote a return letter.

"Dear George, Thank you for your letter which at least puts things straight between us. All I can say is thank God I didn't marry you when you were pressing so hard. You might have pulled out at the first sign of trouble and then where would I have been? As it is, I have my beautiful house, paid for with my own money, and my thriving business which, I think, will thrive even more after the fashion parade on Friday night. We're different types, you and me. Your type sticks together in the end. But I don't care, I'm glad I found out now. It'll be back to the wee ten bob tarts for you then? As to that pressing matter, I'll act on my own behalf. There are other lawyers. Yours sincerely, Maisie Gifford."

* * *

Cora was sitting at her desk in the Latin class. She had felt more and more since the trial that her schoolroom friends had turned against her. Miss Geddes looked ill. She was obviously doing her best to control herself.

"When we consider Caesar's account of the civil war in the Empire," said Miss Geddes, "we must . . . we must make due allowances for his own . . . for his own particular bias." The teacher tried to laugh. "Just as one of you might write an account in the school magazine about a meeting on the sports field with Arbour School, or St. Anne's, and might . . . you might be inclined to describe St. Elizabeth's performance more . . . more charitably that it ought to be described, so Caesar . . ."

Miss Geddes suddenly stopped and walked to the window. The whole class, subdued, looked at her trying to control herself. She turned to them again and started, "So Caesar . . . would overdo his triumphs perhaps." She stopped talking and, for a long moment, looked at the class. They could see that she had lost the thread. Cora could not look at Miss Geddes.

The teacher's mind started to wander. "I've lost the . . . oh, dear . . . I'm getting on, you know. I'm sixty-two. Sixty-two – that's a great age – to you, anyway. Though my father, who lives with me, is eighty-seven. Really, he's a bit of a worry these days, too . . ."

She started to cry. And, as Miss Geddes went on crying, Cora put her head down on the desk. The lesson was over. She went back to the House on the Hill reluctantly.

The moment tea was over, her mother took her into the fitting room and started pinning her into the dress she had specially made for the big fashion show. "They've said you can get up and show it in the parade on Friday – did you know that?"

"I'm not sure I should go," said Cora. Maisie looked at her incredulously. Cora hurried on, "Well, there's the examinations. I should be working."

"You'll walk through them," said Masie. "You're brilliant – they said so. English, French, Latin –"

"Latin's going to be tricky."

"Why?" demanded Maisie. Cora looked straight at her mother. She said deliberately, "They say Miss Geddes is going to resign. She's going off her head, so she's leaving. What a time to lose a good teacher . . ."

"Who said she was a good teacher? The court didn't think she was a very good teacher."

"Are you going to make a fuss about it?" asked Cora fearfully.

"I may have to," announced Maisie, but she could not meet Cora's eyes. "If she's going off her head, it's from a guilty conscience. She knows she was in the wrong. I've got the court to back me up. They have to learn that if they make people suffer, they must pay for it."

Cora was in despair. All she'd wanted to do was to take a gentle rise out of Miss Geddes and get the adulation of the other girls. She had never thought it would end like this.

Next morning when she went to St. Elizabeth's, she found how unpopular she was. A netball game was in progress and she sat there, in her gym clothes, without being asked to take part. All of a sudden she caught sight of her mother crossing over to the school entrance. When Maisie went in without seeing her, Cora rose and shouted, "Who's coming off to give me a turn?"

The girls went on playing as if they hadn't heard her.

It was worse when the playground session was over. All of a sudden, all the girls disappeared and Cora was left to wander disconsolately back to the classroom. When she got there she found the other girls gathered in a corner, whispering and laughing, "*There* you are," she cried. "Whose daring idea was it to come back up the fire escape? No one told me –"

The girls ignored her. She walked to her desk just as a teacher came in. Everyone settled to take out their books for the next lesson. Cora lifted the lid of her desk and saw, in big white letters on the underside, the word "Scum".

Meanwhile her mother was facing the headmistress. Miss Holroyd wore her customary calm look. She was even smiling. "It's so kind of you to come at such short notice," she said. "About your letter to the board of Governors –"

"It wasn't addressed to you," said Maisie sharply.

"No, of course not," said Miss Holroyd and her smile seemed to widen. "But naturally the chairman showed it to me – since it concerns me so intimately."

"You think it's funny?"

Miss Holroyd's smile vanished. "I think it's absurd. It would be funny if the whole affair had not had such a lowering effect on Miss Geddes."

"Miss Geddes has got what she deserved," Maisie was vehement.

"I'd hoped to ask you to persuade her to stay." Maisie looked at the headmistress incredulously. "Mrs. Gifford," said Miss Holroyd, "I understand the strain you've been under, but I wonder if you've considered what's happening to Cora within the school?"

"Do you mean you're victimising her?" demanded Maisie.

"How dare you?" Miss Holroyd spoke the words quietly. "You realise I could insist on her being removed?"

Maisie started shouting. "You've no good reason.

Think of the publicity if you did. Cora will be fine when you've resigned too. I'll prosecute – for negligence – think of the Sheriff's critical remarks."

Miss Holroyd said icily, "The Chairman of the Governors will write to the newspapers regretting those critical remarks and defending me and my excellent record here. You'll make a fool of yourself and a failure of your daughter."

Maisie felt she would burst. She grabbed her handbag and marched out of the room. Miss Holroyd watched her go, then looked up the telephone directory and rang Mrs. Ramsay, who started gushing as soon as she heard the headmistress's voice. Miss Holroyd came straight to the point. Poor Miss Geddes was leaving because she was too ill to continue teaching. She asked Mrs. Ramsay if she would take on fund-raising for a presentation to Miss Geddes.

"It'll be a pleasure and an honour," said a delighted Mrs. Ramsay. She paused for a moment and added, "We all suspect who's to blame."

"I don't wish to talk about blame," said Miss Holroyd.

The headmistress put down the 'phone and permitted herself a faint smile.

* * *

It was the great night – the night of the mannequin show where Maisie's dresses were to be displayed. Her big success was to be Cora. She had made a beautiful dress for the girl, but now that her daughter was wearing it, she felt doubtful. "Come into the light," she said. "Turn around." She looked at the effect. "What do you think?" she asked Cora.

Gracelessly her daughter answered, "The colour's good."

Maisie didn't really hear what she said. She plucked at

the front of the skirt. "Something a wee bit wrong here," she said. "You've filled out."

Cora looked at her mother coldly. "Perhaps I'm pregnant," she said, and started to unbutton her dress. "I'm not going to the show."

"Don't you dare!" Maisie shouted.

Cora shouted back. "They used to like me. They thought I was funny and clever." She choked, stood up and stepped out of the dress. "They used to like me, but you made them hate me!" She ran out of the fitting room and upstairs. Maisie heard the slamming of her bedroom door.

At the mannequin show the Ladies Circle was all agog. In the wings they paraded about in the dresses designed by Maisie Gifford, congratulating each other. Mrs. Ramsay, as usual, was the centre of attraction. She always tried to make sure she was. "Isn't this an absolute triumph?" she cried to Mrs. Milne. "I'm not sure the unemployed deserve it."

Mrs. Milne paid no attention to her. "Everyone in line, please," she ordered. "And I think we might stop giggling."

At that moment Maisie appeared. Mrs. Milne turned towards the stage and Maisie followed her. "Cora's not here," she explained to Mrs. Milne's back. "You know how it is," she heard herself stammering, "these young girls . . . Your dress looks awfully well, I must say . . ."

She started towards the amateur mannequins, when Mrs. Ramsay said bluntly, "The fact is, we're all behind Miss Holroyd." Maisie was taken aback. Mrs. Milne, in the dress she had designed for her, took the stage and said, "As you probably know, economy has been our theme in this year's effort. The members of the Ladies Circle have decided to mount their very own fashion show. Their very own in the sense that the dresses you will see are all owned by the wearers."

Maisie was bewildered. She had made most of the dresses. She blurted out to the women in the wings, "Miss Holroyd and Miss Geddes caused harm to my daughter. They broke the rules. They've to pay for that. They could do it to your daughters next."

Mrs. Milne was addressing the fashionable audience. "All we'd like you to remember," she said archly, "is that we're not professional mannequins." She started to introduce Mrs. Ramsay but Maisie, now beside herself, grabbed hold of the lady. "This is *my* fashion show," she shouted. She tugged at Mrs. Ramsay's dress. "I made this." She was almost incoherent with rage. "Sticking together, are you? All good friends, eh? Well, I'll tell you this – you're no different from anyone else – because I've seen you with your clothes off."

Mrs. Milne's introduction had fallen flat. She walked off the stage, took in the situation, and beckoned to an attendant. Maisie had lost control altogether. She was shouting incoherently. The attendant grabbed hold of her arm and led her out. Her sobs disappeared into the distance. Mrs. Ramsay looked pleased. "That's that," she said to Mrs. Milne. "On with the show."

And that was the end of Maisie Gifford, fashionable modiste. Once again the House on the Hill was empty. Maisie stood in the now bare fitting room and looked out of the window. George Barton stood beside her. "There's no need for any of this," he said.

Maisie turned to him. "There's no work coming in. I can't keep the house if there's no work. It's not a bad place I've got in Sturmer Crescent."

"You know what I mean – there's my house."

"No," said Maisie forcibly. But as she expressed her

defiance in her voice, she quaked inwardly. Could she – it seemed impossible – but could she be wrong?

George seemed to sense her doubt. "What about Cora?" he asked.

"Cora's back at Eastfield School. She says she's away to the teachers' training college in Aberdeen in the autumn. That's if she passes her examinations."

"She'll pass," George said confidently. He realised that this was not the indomitable Maisie he had known.

Maisie shook her head. "I don't know – they say her nerves may let her down. She worries me."

"I'm away then," said George. He was about to open the door when the bell rang. When he opened it, there was the rag-and-bone man's little girl on the doorstep. She looked as disreputable as ever but her big smile came through the grime.

"My da says ta for the big bundle," the dirty wee girl said. "An' we're sorry you're going away."

She ran down the stairs and jumped on the piled high cart. The rag-and-bone man looked up and waved goodbye to Maisie. She couldn't tell why, but the tears came to her eyes. She wiped them away with the back of her hand and looked round. George was not away. He was standing in the empty hall, forlorn and miserable. A great pity for the rest of the world suddenly filled Maisie. She went towards him.

# 1944
# SOMETHING for the BOYS

# Something For The Boys · 1944

It was the year 1944. The whole world seemed to be fighting. Britain, left seemingly alone after the disaster of Dunkirk, now had the two most formidable allies in the world – Soviet Russia and the United States of America. But Germany and Japan were still powerful opponents and, although Italy seemed to be lagging, its forces had at the very least a nuisance value.

Glasgow was one of the greatest centres of wartime activity in the United Kingdom. The shipyards on the River Clyde were actually building and repairing more ships than all of the American shipyards put together. The pride of the Clyde, the two giant liners, Queen Mary and Queen Elizabeth, were acting as Atlantic ferries, bringing across men, munitions and material (including much needed food) from the United States. The liners docked at Greenock and the first thing the G.I.s did was to take the Chattanooga choo-choo to Glasgow. Glasgow was their Mecca, even in the black-out and with rationed food and, maybe what was worse, severely restricted whisky supplies. In Glasgow pubs you could get only beer to drink, until the manager blew a whistle to indicate that whisky was on sale for five minutes. When he blew the second blast, you'd had your lot.

The city was full of Sassenachs, which is an affectionate nickname given by the Scots to foreigners. There were the Poles, under General Sikorsky, who had remade his forces in the West of Scotland. There were Norwegians who had escaped from their country when Hitler invaded it. The Free French, grouped under General de Gaulle, were everywhere. Other countries, even Russia, were represented. But by far the biggest number of Sassenachs were the Americans. "Any gum, chum?" was the question asked of them by cheeky wee Glasgow boys who were almost always rewarded with a packet or two.

It wasn't surprising, then, that the House on the Hill had been taken over by the Americans. It was a convenient centre, with a good number of rooms. The drawing room was turned into a lecture hall. The dining room had been remade as a living room-cum-bedroom for the caretaker, a Lancashire lass known to one and all as just Jean. She was in her early thirties, pleasant looking, as well dressed as you could expect in those days of clothes rationing. What was more important, she was a hard-working manager and, what endeared her to visiting Americans, had a sense of humour.

Jean had been on holiday in Blackpool just before the war started and there she met a handsome Glasgow chap. They fell in love, got married, and he took her back to Glasgow and then, when he got a job in the world-famous shipbuilding yard of John Brown's, they went to Clydebank. It was not the most beautiful place in the world but, being used to Lancashire, Jean enjoyed it. She worshipped her big, strong husband and was happy that he could not be called up when the war started because he was in a reserved, essential job. There were, of course, all the worries of wartime but there were good points too.

True, there were the frequent air-raid alerts, but they seldom amounted to anything more than the discomfort of sitting up all night in an air-raid shelter. And you did get used to the black-out and wearing old clothes and eating Spam, because there wasn't much else to eat. Jean reflected on the troubles of the Londoners and other people in the South of England who were being bombed all the time. Even as far north as Lancashire there were air raids. Scotland seemed to be lucky. Some people said it was because of the mountains and sometimes, when they went for a holiday trip to Loch Lomond or down the river to the Firth of Clyde, Jean would look at the towering mountains and inwardly bless them. In any case, as she often reminded herself, you could get used to anything. She had her man and that was that.

Her husband was a great chap for quoting the works of Robert Burns. Jean couldn't understand most of those Scotch words but, if it was "Tam o' Shanter" that he was quoting, she did understand –

"But pleasures are like poppies spread:
You seize the flow'r, its bloom is shed . . ."

And so there came the night of the Bombers' Moon over Clydebank. The air raid sirens sounded, the optimistic stayed where they were, the pessimistic went into the shelters. And then all hell was let loose. The Nazi bombers were concentrating on Clydebank. Jean shivered in the shelter while her husband did his job as an air-raid warden outside. All round about her there were terrible explosions and the roar of flames as the incendiary bombs dropped. In the early hours of the morning the bombing stopped and her husband came back filthy and tired. He said he'd better go down to John Brown's yard but he didn't know what had happened there. He had heard that a French warship in the Clyde had blown up, and there were fires burning everywhere in Clydebank.

On the next night the Bombers' Moon was shining again. As the sirens wailed, Jean saw her husband collect his helmet and his gas-mask and trudge wearily out. She never saw him again. The big shipbuilding town of Clydebank was virtually knocked flat. It was said that there were only nine houses left undamaged in the whole place. When the All Clear sounded, Jean went out and walked through the ruined, burning streets, looking for her husband. She never discovered what had happened to him.

What to do now? She couldn't stay in Clydebank, although the shipbuilders who had survived the bombing were going back to the yard, which miraculously was untouched. The only thing to do was to go to Glasgow, where the bombing had been bad but mainly in the Western suburbs between the city and Clydebank.

And that was how she came to be caretaker for the Americans in the House on the Hill. She was glad to get the job. It helped to take her mind off the dreadful death of her husband. She felt herself to be a survivor and realised that the most important thing in her life was to keep surviving. So she welcomed her place in the dining room and got the Yanks to instal a Morrison shelter there. She also welcomed her share of the American Army food.

The strange thing was that the Americans did not seem to find any use for the big basement. All the rooms from the ground floor up were used. Indeed, sometimes Jean felt there was enough food in the House on the Hill to feed – well, maybe not Glasgow, but at least Edinburgh. She went down into the basement and looked round the huge kitchen and, as they said in the advertisements, all the adjacent offices. And it was then that she had her idea. Why not turn the basement into a wee club for servicemen?

She cleaned the place out and put in some tables and chairs and a basic form of decoration. Nobody was expecting much with a war on. She bought a second-hand gramophone and some popular records of the day. She brought in material for a little bar and at one end of it installed a cash box. Next she had to find supplies of drink and drink, as I have indicated, was difficult to get in Glasgow in 1944.

Jean examined the American Servicemen coming in and out all day. The man who looked after the food supplies was a Sergeant Ellwood. Jean was very popular with the boys and Sergeant Ellwood was a regular visitor.

One afternoon, when he came in to supervise a delivery and smelled of drink, Jean felt that the time was ripe. She explained her idea of a servicemen's club in the basement and he approved immediately. So she put it to him delicately that she would need supplies of alcoholic drink, and even non-alcoholic drink. Sergeant Ellwood was charmed with the idea. In his rich Texan drawl he assured her that she had come to the right man. "Anything for the boys", was his patriotic motto. It was possible, of course, to siphon off some of the Coke, 7 UP, and similar essential additives from existing stock in the house, but he agreed that he would be responsible for the supply of hard liquor which he could obtain from various sources which he did not name.

And so something for the boys was started in the basement of the House on the Hill. Word got around Americans that there was this special place above Kelvingrove Park. Jean soon found that she had to engage two stalwart helpers. One was Jon, an ex-welterweight boxer. He was appointed as doorkeeper, a very important appointment indeed, because it was essential that no one who might cause trouble should get in. The other was Luigi, the first Welsh Italian whom Jean had ever met. He was the barman, but he was also ready for trouble.

Jon screened everyone at the cellar door. Usually he had no doubt whatever as to whether a customer should be let in or not. But occasionally he did doubt and his duty then was to seek Jean's advice. Jean, however, discovered as the club got going, that there was remarkably little to worry about. Word seemed to spread around not only the American Forces and the British but the Allied Forces as well. At first Jean allowed women into the basement, but she soon found this was a mistake. It should be a male – if that was the right word – sodality. The boys all got on well together. Women, apart from Jean of course, seemed to cause trouble.

And so, every evening, Jean put on make-up, which she didn't use during the day, dressed in the best clothes she could get in wartime, and acted as a charming but eagle-eyed hostess and, most important of all, as the cashier.

* * *

It was a pleasant spring morning, and Jean looked out over the park which was turning refreshingly green. She turned from the window and went back to her cooker in the corner. It was breakfast time. She had just lit the gas when the bell rang. She hastily turned it off and went to the door. Two G.I.s stood there, a big packing case between them and an American Army jeep on the terrace behind them.

"Your favourite man," announced a brash young man. Mid-West, Jean decided. She was getting accustomed to their funny accents.

"Not at this time in the morning you're not," she said.

"Is that a welcome?" asked the G.I. aggrievedly. "And I told Joe here you'd be all smiles."

"I can't manage a smile till after breakfast."

As they lifted the crate and brought it in, the Mid-West private said, "She's not usually this way, Joe. She's usually the sweetest, prettiest, most charming –"

"And that cuts no ice with me," announced Jean. "You ought to know it by now – you've tried it before." She gestured towards the crate. "You'll have to take it upstairs."

"Oh, no," moaned Mid-West.

"Every room down here is full," Jean stated. "Go on – it can't be that heavy. Put your backs into it."

"Can't we leave it down here?" The second G.I. sounded like someone from the Deep South. Jean said, "You know very well you can't. Now get up these stairs and stop moaning."

The two boys lifted the crate and started up the stairs. Jean went into her room and noted the new delivery. As she did, she glanced at the appointments section and suddenly realised that there was to be a lecture in ten minutes in the drawing room. Breakfast was out. All she had time for was a cup of coffee. Thank God, the American coffee was stronger than the wishy-washy stuff sold in Britain these days.

She drank her coffee quickly and crossed to the drawing room. She sometimes wondered what it had looked like in the good old days. Now it looked like a public office. The walls were decorated with U.S. Army Information posters, and on a trestle table by the window was a screen for showing slides. Jean plugged in the slide projector just as a loud American voice (definitely New York) shouted from the hall, "Sorry I'm late."

In came an American Army Captain who, even in his uniform, looked as though he was more accustomed to selling insurance. He looked round the empty chairs and asked, "I am in the right place? I'm supposed to be lecturing to twenty-nine enlisted men at this address."

"Oh, yes," said Jean. "This is the right place."

"Where are they?" demanded the Captain.

"They're late," explained Jean a thought wearily. "They often are. They usually leave it to the last minute, the First Army."

The Captain had no time for idle badinage. He strode purposefully to the screen. "Don't let me delay you," he dismissed Jean. "Everything here seems fine." He opened his briefcase and extracted a box of slides.

"It's what we usually have," explained Jean.

"Yes," barked the Captain. He was used to dealing with the lower orders. "When they arrive, if you could direct them in here immediately. My time is at a premium today." Jean was about to leave when the Captain added, "Oh, and I shall need someone to operate the projector. Is he late as well?"

"No, said Jean, "that'll be me."

The Captain was startled. "You?" he asked incredulously. "I don't think . . ." His voice trailed off.

"I can do it," Jean reassured him. "We're always having these lectures. You just have to let me know when to change the slides. Some people like to cough, some stamp their foot and some tap a cane. Whichever way you like – it doesn't matter to me."

"No, you don't understand," said the Captain in a pained voice. "The subject matter of this particular lecture is, shall we say, a little – well, more than a little – indelicate. For a lady."

"It's not *The Evils of Prostitution*, is it?" asked Jean brightly. "We had that a month ago."

"No, it is not. My topic is of a medical nature. Though perhaps it isn't – well, totally unrelated to what you mention."

Jean nodded understandingly. "Well, are these them?" she asked, picking up the box of slides.

"But, Mrs. –"

"Black," said Jean, crossing to the projector.

"Mrs. Black, some of these slides are – well – very explicit. Strong men have been known to –"

"Don't you worry about me, Captain," said Jean.

"You'd do better wondering where your audience is."

The brash Captain looked suddenly crestfallen. Jean felt sorry for him. She looked up at the ceiling and had an idea.

On the top floor of the House on the Hill the two G.I.s were in one of the former bedrooms. They had stowed their crate along with the others which were nearly filling the room. But they were in no hurry to leave.

"Nice old house this," said one. "Shame it's just a dump for what we can't store on base." He lifted his head. "Hey, does she live here alone?"

"I guess so," said the G.I. who had announced himself as Jean's favourite man.

"Maybe she gets lonely at nights? Sitting down below, pining for company."

"Didn't you look?" His companion pointed at the third finger of his left hand. "She's married."

"I heard they wear those sometimes just to put us off. Come on, let's try being nice to her. If we get in her good books, this could be the cosiest little nest in town."

In the drawing-room, now lecture room, Jean was listening. "I don't understand this," said the Captain to her. "Where can the enlisted men be?" Jean heard footsteps on the stairs and rose. "Excuse me, Captain," she said.

In the hall, sure enough, were the two G.I.s. "Still here, boys?" she asked brightly.

"How could we leave without collecting your autograph?" said the first G.I. He handed her the delivery note and a pen.

The second G.I. cleared his throat and observed, "You sure keep a tidy place, ma'am. Isn't it a lot for just one?" He nudged his friend, who immediately asked, "Say, no chance of a coffee round here, is there?"

Jean looked up from signing the delivery note and

nodded. "And I bet you wouldn't say no to a slice of fruit slab to go with it?"

The two Americans were delighted. "That'd be great!" said the new man. "Didn't I tell you, Joe?" cried his friend. "She is the sweetest –"

Jean interrupted. "Well, I'll see what I can do," she said. "First of all, though, would you just do something for me?"

Before they knew what had happened, she had taken them by the arm and led them across the hall into the lecture room. The Captain's eyes brightened as he saw them. Jean ushered them into seats, went back and put the lights out, and took her seat to operate the projector. The title slide was on the screen. It read simply, *V.D. and You.* The Captain started to give his lecture and, as one slide followed another, his audience of two began to look at the floor or anywhere except at the screen. When the lights went on, they did not wait for coffee and fruit slab. They bolted to their jeep.

* * *

Jean was a methodical person. Indeed, her husband had always been complimenting her on the way she "arranged" things. She was absorbed in arranging now. Some day, perhaps, the Americans would decide to use the basement and then her pleasant and nicely run club for the boys would come to a sudden end. In the meantime, her one worry was what the neighbours might think. The fact that soldiers, sailors and airmen went in and out of the place at night could be explained, but the occasional noise was a worry to Jean. And today she had her nearest neighbour, Mrs. McDonald, in for a cup of tea. Mrs. McDonald's husband had been called up and was now away in London doing his bit in the Army Kinematograph Service.

"And how's Mr. McDonald?" asked Jean solicitously, as she poured her guest's first cup of tea.

"We've had a letter," said Mrs. McDonald solemnly. "He's well, thank God."

"Good. And things in general?"

"Not *too* bad."

Jean grew suddenly grave. She leaned over to Mrs. McDonald and said in a low tone, "Did you hear it last night?"

Mrs. McDonald was taken aback. "Well, as I've said to you before, I'm a very light sleeper."

Jean looked as if she might break down. "Oh, Mrs. McDonald," she appealed, "you've got to help me. I don't think I can go on."

"What is it?" asked her guest anxiously. "Don't upset yourself."

"It's not the regular work, the eight till six – I can cope with that. It's these special meetings they're having night after night."

"Calm down now, calm down," soothed Mrs. McDonald.

"But what can I do?" cried Jean. "I'm working through till midnight every night and it's too much. Oh, I know there's a war on. And I know a lot of very important Top Secret Planning gets done in these late-night sessions. But it's wearing me into the ground!"

"Something will have to be done. You'll have to complain."

"I've done that," protested Jean. "It's no use."

"Then we'll all have to complain," pronounced Mrs. McDonald. "After all, this is a residential area, war or no war. These visitors to our shores will have to learn to be quiet. Voices at that time of night, sometimes high girlish laughter – it's very disturbing."

Jean shook her head. "I told them last night. I said to

the Captain, 'You must be quiet when you leave', I said. 'People are sleeping round here.' Do you know what he said to me? He said, 'It's so people can rest peacefully in their beds at night, without fear or threat, that we are having these meetings'."

Mrs. McDonald looked impressed. Jean leaned over to her and whispered, "I mean, I don't intrude, but . . . I think it's the Second Front they're planning."

"Is that right?"

"So what could I say? When there's work of that – that magnitude on, you don't like to carp about a few hours lost sleep." Jean gave a resigned shrug. "What can we do but grin and bear it for the duration? Of course, I'm paid for it, but I was far more worried about you being disturbed."

Mrs. McDonald actually permitted herself a smile. "Oh, don't you worry yourself on that score," she said. "Not now you've told me. I'm prepared to turn a blind eye. Or, shall we say, a deaf ear?"

They giggled together at Mrs. McDonald's little joke and Jean said, "Oh, Mrs. McDonald, I do like having our little chats."

Mrs. McDonald rose and said ponderously, "That's what neighbours are for."

Jean went to her sideboard and produced a small, covered bowl. "Before you go," she said, "I wonder if you could use these?"

She unveiled pineapple rings, which were almost unobtainable in Glasgow at that time.

"Oh, no," protested Mrs. McDonald, automatically. "I couldn't."

"Go on," encouraged Jean. "I've had all I want and I'd like you to have them."

"Well, if you're sure . . ." smiled Mrs. McDonald.

And Jean smiled in return.

* * *

There were two men converging on the House on the Hill that night. One was a young Glasgow soldier, on leave, who had heard about the place and had already, that morning reconnoitred it. He'd fixed the house when the American jeep drove up and the two G.I.s came out with the big parcel. Then he'd gone straight back home to Maryhill and eventually had high tea with his mother and father. His name was Dougie Morrison and he had already seen much more of the war than he wanted. What he did want was something he found hard to define. But the stories he had been told about this house on the hill appealed to him in one way, while he tried to reject the appeal in another.

After tea he came into the small tenement living room and saw his mother sitting by the fire with her purse already in her hand. "I'm off now," he said.

His mother looked at him. "Your dad was hoping you'd go to the pub with him," she reproved.

"I'll do that another night," said Dougie. "This is just my first night back." He saw his mother opening her purse. "Aw, don't do that," he said.

"Do what?" said Mrs. Morrison, seeming bewildered.

Dougie was not taken in. "You're going to give me money – I know you are. I don't need it. I've got my pay."

"First time I've ever known you refuse half-a-crown for an evening out," said his mother. "Don't you want it?"

"I don't need it," said Dougie, almost roughly. "I'm not a kid to come running to you for pennies out your purse. I'm going."

"When will you be back?"

"I don't know. Late. I'll let myself in."

"Aren't you forgetting something?" asked Mrs. Morrison and, when Dougie shook his head, she said, "You'll need the key." She took the key from her purse, together with a half-crown.

"Maw!" ejaculated Dougie, but he took the key and the half-crown and they smiled at each other. He said good night and started walking from Maryhill to the House on the Hill.

The other man whose immediate destination was exactly the same address was an American soldier of their First Army – Sergeant Frank Rhodes, known for obvious nickname reasons as Dusty. He arrived in Glasgow's Central Station and immediately saw the huge notice advertising all the places in the city catering to servicemen, especially visiting servicemen. He had heard of Glasgow's welcome reputation, but he found it rather too much to take in at one glance. As he was still trying to absorb the glut of information, a man, lookingly somehow furtive, approached him. "Hey, chum," said this man. "D'you want to buy some whisky?"

"I don't think so," said Dusty.

"It's good stuff," said the man. "The best you can get. For this quality it's usually a fiver. Ask anyone. But for you, 'cos of the great job you Yanks are doing, four pounds ten shillings."

Dusty didn't think a great deal of this offer, but the man said, "I'm cutting my own throat, but nothing's too good for you boys. What d'you say?"

"I say O.K.," said Dusty, and the man stuffed the bottle into Dusty's kitbag. "First time here, is it?" he asked.

"First time," responded Dusty.

"I'd like to show you round a bit, but I'm running for a train." Dusty pulled out his wallet and handed over the money. The man disappeared rapidly. Dusty turned back to the big board with all the notices of accommodation. He picked the American Red Cross Club in what had been the Grand Hotel at Charing Cross. When he got there, he was shown into a fair-sized bedroom which had four beds in it. He picked the least rumpled bed, sat down and took out his newly acquired whisky bottle. First of all he found that he could get nothing out of it. Then he looked into the bottle and could see a film of wax. He took a pen and jabbed at it. Liquid appeared and Dusty raised the bottle to his lips and took a quick swig. The taste was so terrible that he immediately sprayed it out of his mouth. He knew he had been conned and threw the rest of the bottle, with its contents, into a wastepaper bin.

He'd been told by his Army friends so much about Glasgow that he could hardly believe what had happened. Glasgow was the great place where everybody was friendly. And now what? Well, he had the address in – what was it called? – Park Terrace. He'd give that a tumble. In any case, he had to be back in Liverpool next morning so, if this was another disappointment, there was not much skin off his nose. He set off to walk the fairly short distance from the American Red Cross Club to the House on the Hill.

He found the address, went down the basement steps and gave what he had been told was the proper arrangement of knocks. The door was eventually opened by a big, surly man. Dusty said, "Hi!" but there was no reply. "What's the matter?" said the American Sergeant. "Didn't I do the knock right?"

Jon wasted no words. "From Greenock?" he demanded. Dusty shook his head. "Bellahouston Park?" "No," said Dusty. Jon said "Sorry" and started to close the door.

"I've come all the way from Liverpool," said Dusty pleadingly.

A strong female voice at the back of the corridor said, "Let him in, Jon." The door was held wide open and in went Dusty to see this very self-possessed, well-dressed woman appraising him. "All the way from Liverpool?" she said. "Word certainly gets about."

"You were highly recommended," said Dusty.

"I hope you're not disappointed," replied Jean, as she showed him into the club for the boys. Dusty's eyes registered the black-out curtains on the basement windows, decorated with silver stars, the half dozen or so tables, each with a candle burning, and a gas oven, with both doors open, which was obviously the source of heat for the room. There was a gramophone playing *Stardust*.

Sergeant Rhodes looked around at the members of the club in attendance. At the nearest table sat two airmen, an American and a Pole, deep in conversation. Two American Army men sat at the next table, engrossed in each other. Three British Army privates were embracing each other and drinking a toast of some kind. In the middle of the floor, completely unregarded by the others, was an American Sergeant dancing with an R.A.F. officer. And at one table sat a Scottish soldier, morosely alone. Dusty's eyes fell upon him.

His thoughts, or, to put it practically, thought was broken for a moment when Jean, now very much the manageress and sitting behind the cash box, enquired, "Well, what would you like?"

Dusty asked for gin. "Give him a gin, Luigi," said Jean. "Now, there's two things I ask of newcomers here. Please make no noise at all when you're leaving."

"Sure," Dusty assured her.

"And don't go shooting your mouth off about this place. A word to the wise is all right, but no more than that. Or you may find we're not in business the next time you want to come. Savvy?"

Sergeant Dusty Rhodes took his drink and said, "I understand."

"Good," said Jean with a bright smile. "I hope you enjoy your evening and that'll be one-and-six."

The gramophone record ended and the two men who were dancing together returned to their table, jostling the single Scottish soldier as they squeezed in. Dusty observed that this man was nervous and ill at ease, and covering it up by being aggressive. He made his mind up and approached the lonely man at the table.

"Is this seat taken?" he enquired.

Dougie Morrison didn't even look up. "No," he grunted.

"Mind if I join you?" asked Dusty.

"No," grunted Dougie again. But immediately he got up, went to the bar and ordered another drink. Dusty loosened his uniform jacket, lit a cigarette and looked round. As Dougie returned with his drink, Dusty said, "Is this crowded or does it get better later?"

"Don't know," said Dougie and took a pull at his drink.

"Not a regular?" asked Dusty. Dougie indicated he wasn't. "My first time," said Dusty easily. "A friend told me about it, I had a leave coming up, and here I am. Smoke?" Dougie shook his head. "Yeah," said Dusty. "I got forty-eight hours. Well, I have had twenty-four of them. What about you?"

Dougie still looked surly, but replied, "A fortnight."

"Wow!" cried Dusty. "What did you do – win a medal?" Dougie still didn't say a word and Dusty said, "You must have been somewhere pretty hot."

"Africa," said Dougie flatly.

Dusty persevered. "Yeah, I guess that's pretty hot. I'm still in combat training, but we'll hear soon where we're posted. They say it's toughest before they ship you out and, brother, it's really bad now." He pulled back the sleeve of his uniform jacket and showed a bandage. "Gashed my arm on exercises, crawling through barbed wire. Thought I was going to bleed to death in camp and never get to France."

"That'd be a tragedy," said Dougie and Dusty's eyebrows went up. "I mean, if you didn't get over there and win the war for us."

Dusty shook his head. "I think somebody sold me a pile of garbage when they told me how friendly the Scots were."

"You're still in training," Dougie was scornful. "You've seen nothing." He immediately regretted his words. After a pause he looked at Dusty and said, "My name's Douglas Morrison."

The other put out his hand. "Frank Rhodes – but everybody calls me Dusty." They shook hands. "Sorry," said Dougie. "It's this place. I'm not used to it." They started talking intimately about peace-time life and what had happened since. Dusty, a man of the world as far as this kind of situation was concerned, led the conversation in the way he wanted. Soon he had Dougie telling about his special friend in the Army. "He was married," he explained. "And he was very, very faithful to her. He wouldn't go out with the other lads. He always stuck with me."

Dusty encouraged him and then, when he calculated that the time was ripe, said, "How'd you like to dance with me?" Dougie looked horrified. "Come on," said Dusty. "Let's take a little twirl around the floor. Man to man." He was clowning a bit, but Dougie was not responding. Dusty became serious. "Do you live with your folks?" he asked. Dougie nodded.

"I don't see them in here tonight," said Dusty. He looked straight at the Scot and said, "You're in a club, Dougie. You joined it the minute you walked in here. You may as well start acting like a member. It's a lot more fun."

Dougie rose. "I'll get us some drinks," he said.

"Okay," said Dusty, still looking directly at him. "And if the lady with the gramophone is doing requests, ask her for the *I-Yi-Yi-Yi-Yi* song. The one that goes *I like you very much.*"

As Dougie returned with the drinks he nodded towards the bar. "Hey," he said, "she's a big girl." Dusty looked at the figure talking to Jean. He started laughing, then said to Dougie, "'She' is a man." Dougie looked at the visitor again and drank quickly to hide his embarrassment.

"You're blushing," bantered Dusty. And as Dougie denied it, Dusty added, "There's nothing wrong with it. I think it's . . . cute."

"Oh, Christ, don't *say* that." Dougie made a grimace. "Next thing I know you'll be calling me 'honey'."

"How old are you, Dougie?" asked Dusty smoothly.

"Twenty-four. Why?"

Dusty leaned over towards him. "And how long have you known about yourself?"

Dougie met his gaze. "Aw, a while," he answered.

"And how long's that?"

Dougie pondered a moment. "Well . . . ten years or more."

"And you haven't got used to the idea yet?"

The whole situation between the couple had changed. They were friends now and they talked quietly together. Suddenly Dougie asked, "What time is it?" "On eleven," Dusty consulted his watch.

Dougie cleared his throat. "When . . . ah . . . when do you have to get back?"

"Train tomorrow morning. Eight fifteen."

"You'll be wanting a good night's rest," there was a question in Dougie's statement.

"You should see the room I've got. It's small, cramped and I'll probably have to share it with three drunks." It was Dusty's turn to clear his throat. "What are your plans for tonight?" he asked. "Your folks waiting up for you? I'll walk you home. I could do with some fresh air."

"It's too far," said Dougie.

"What else are you going to do – if you don't go home?"

"Don't know," said Dougie.

Dusty leaned towards him. "How do you feel about committing a crime?"

"I'd like to very much," said Dougie. "Thanks."

Jean said goodbye to her 'lady' friend at the bar, looked at the time, and was now walking round the tables calling, "Drink up now, please, gents. Nearly closing time." Dusty looked at her thoughtfully. "She may know somewhere," he said. Before Dougie could object, he got up to join Jean, who was switching off the burners in the oven. Dougie tried to pretend that the happening wasn't happening.

Dusty was saying to Jean, "So, you can see our problem." As Jean nodded, he urged, "If you know of anyone who can let us have a room. I mean, I'll pay, of course – just as long as they understand. Do you know of anywhere?"

Jean looked over at the lonely Dougie. She smiled and looked up and nodded towards the ceiling.

* * *

Carrying her cashbox as a mother carries her baby, Jean took them up from the basement. "I wouldn't like you to go getting the wrong idea," she said. "It's not a refuge for waifs and strays." She looked at Dougie. "But when I saw your face – well, that did it. This is where I live. Come in for a night-cap." She led the way into the dining room, and poured port into a glass and two cups. As they drank the port, Dusty carried on the conversation with Jean. Dougie said not a word.

"You'll want to go to bed," said Jean at last. As she collected her keys from the mantelpiece she assured them, "The room's nice. It's about the only one left here that is. I have to keep it that way in case the Army have any V.I.P.s over on a visit."

"We both fit in to that category?" smiled Dusty.

"Well, tonight you do," Jean smiled back, and led the way up to the best bedroom. Dusty looked round the nicely furnished room with appreciation. It was so different from the rest of the house. Dougie didn't appear to notice the difference. He kept his eyes on the carpet.

"Sweet dreams," said Jean and shut the door behind her.

Immediately Dougie went to the door, then turned round almost accusingly. "There's no lock," he said.

"What do you want a lock for?" Dusty enquired.

"To be private. She might come in."

"Why should she?" Dusty demanded. "She's going to bed. Like we are." He leapt on to the bed and bounced in delight. "Hey," he cried, "this is all right." He stretched out with his arms behind his head. "Ah!" he breathed, "isn't this romantic?" He jumped up purposefully. "Sack-time, I think," he said as he took off his jacket and tie." He looked at Dougie, who still appeared to be studying the carpet. "Are you getting undressed?"

Dougie sat down and slowly took his Army boots off. Dusty shook his head and said quietly, "Come here." As Dougie rose and came towards him Dusty put his hands on the Scottish soldier's shoulders. "Okay?" he asked.

"'Course," muttered Dougie.

"You're stiff as a board," said Dusty, and then suddenly, "Are you a virgin, Dougie?"

Dougie shook his head. Then he looked straight at Dusty. "Yes," he said. He paused and added, "I'm sorry."

"Oh, Dougie – you don't have to be sorry. Why didn't you tell me before?"

"I didn't like."

"But why not?" Dusty's expression was incredulous.

"Well, it's ridiculous," Dougie did seem to relax all of a sudden. "You hear all these stories about young girls losing their virginity to G.I.s. And here I am – a grown man – a soldier! And I'm doing the same thing."

Laughing, they threw off their clothes and went to bed.

* * *

Dougie woke up. He couldn't think at first where he was or why he was feeling happy. Then he recognised the bedroom in the House on the Hill. He looked over at Dusty, who was still sleeping. He smiled to himself. There was no need to pretend any longer. Dougie now realised his nature and he felt content to be what he was.

There was a sudden knock at the bedroom door. Dougie panicked. He nudged Dusty's back. "Hey, Dusty," he whispered as loud as he dared. "Dusty, wake up." And, as Dusty surfaced, Dougie said urgently, "There's somebody at the door."

The knock came again and Jean's voice said, "It's only me."

"Dusty," said the still panicked Dougie. "It's her. She wants to come in! What are we going to do?"

Dusty got up on one elbow. "Come in," he called.

"Oh, no!" moaned Dougie and dived beneath the bedclothes.

In came Jean with a tray. "I was up early," she said, "so I brought you a cup of tea." "Thank you," said Dusty, sitting up.

"Sleep all right?" asked Jean, trying to ignore the lump under the bedclothes. Dusty assured her he had.

"It's a lovely morning out," said Jean. "Not cold at all.

Just how it should be for Spring." She looked at the lump in the bed. "Is he awake?" she asked.

"He's awake," answered Dusty. He leaned over and tapped Dougie somewhere on the shoulder. "Hey, Dougie, come on," he said loudly. "Reveille."

As if he were a tortoise coming out at the first sign of Spring, Dougie gradually emerged from the bedclothes. "Hello," he said. "I was asleep." Jean handed him a cup of tea, so he was forced to sit up, but he pulled a bedsheet round him. Jean nodded towards the window. "With much more of this weather we'll be getting a sun-tan." She looked appraisingly at Dusty's chest. "Mind you," she said, "you're brown already, aren't you?"

Dusty glanced complacently down at his chest. "It's wearing off," he complained.

"No, but next to him you are. He looks –" Jean turned to Dougie. "What's that word you use when you mean pale? You know, the Scottish way of saying it."

Dougie gulped. "Peely-wally," he ventured.

"That's it," cried Jean. "Peely-wally. I think its such a funny expression."

"I never heard it," confessed Dusty.

"Nor did I till I came here. It makes me laugh, though. Peely-wally!"

Jean had been sitting on the bed beside Dougie. She rose and said, "Well, I'd better let you get on. You're all right for time – it's just after seven."

She went out and the embarrassed Dougie's head dropped. "Oh, no," he moaned. "I want to die." Dusty raised his eyebrows. "I've never been so embarrassed in my life. Us two, lying here like this, and her sat there on the end of the bed."

"She's seen it all before," said Dusty calmly. "It's nothing new."

"Maybe not to her," Dougie's head still drooped. "It is to me."

Dusty looked at his watch. "My God," he shouted. "Look at the time. My bloody train –"

Fifteen minutes later they were down in the hall. Jean came out with a small parcel, which she handed to Dusty. "I made this up for you," she said. "You'll need something for the journey."

Dusty was touched. "Thanks," he said. "Ah, I left you something on the table. For the room."

"Come on!" shouted Dougie at the door.

"Bye, bye!" cried Jean. "Look after yourselves." She watched them hurrying down the hill.

Dusty and Dougie arrived at Central Station with only a minute or two to spare. As he saw the big noticeboard of advertisements, Dusty smiled and said, "Well, this is where I came in."

"I won't come any further," said Dougie.

"Not going to wave me off?"

"No," said Dougie. "It'd be like that scene in the –"

"In the pictures," Dusty completed it for him." He looked at his friend. "Dougie, at the risk of paying you a compliment, I've had a very nice time. What about you?"

"Yes," said Dougie.

"Glad you met me?"

"Yes," said Dougie.

"Going to kiss me goodbye?"

"No," said Dougie.

"I thought not. How about a quick, brotherly hug?"

They hugged each other. An elderly man passing by said approvingly, "That's what I like to see. The Allies getting on together. Good luck to you, boys. You're doing a grand job."

They stood back from each other. "Be seeing you," said

Dusty, hoisting his kit-bag. Dougie watched him go through the platform entrance.

That night Jean had just opened her club. She was checking the float in her cash-box when she heard someone being admitted by Jon. To her surprise she saw it was the peely-wally Scots soldier. But somehow he didn't seem to be so peely-wally now. "Oh," said Jean, "I wasn't sure I'd be seeing you again."

"You might be seeing quite a bit of me," Dougie had a new-found confidence. "Fortnight's leave."

"Did your friend get away all right?"

"Yes," said Dougie, "I saw him off."

"Nice chap," Jean smiled. "Well, you're early. Do you want one?"

"A whisky, please."

"A whisky, please, Luigi," called Jean to her barman, and then said to Dougie, "You can have that on the house. What he left me for the room . . . well, he was generous, to say the least."

"Thanks," nodded Dougie. "And thanks again for last night."

"Don't mention it. And I mean that – not to a living soul."

Dougie took his glass of whisky, walked straight over to the table where he had sat with Dusty. He felt happy. As he decided that he would spend every night of his leave in this basement in the House on the Hill, he realised that, whatever good or bad followed, this was the moment when, in all senses of the word, he had finally joined the club.

Jean nodded to Luigi to put a record on the gramophone. Luigi took the first one off the pile and flicked on the machine. It was a new song of Cole Porter's – *Something for the Boys*.

# 1980
# NOTHING like a DAME

# Nothing Like a Dame · 1980

The House on the Hill had gradually changed its personality over the years. It had had its ups and downs, but mainly downs. It had had its successes and disasters. Now, from the outside, it looked rather drab. At the front door there were three bells. One was for the ground floor, which was a posh flat. Two other bells marked "Flat 2" and "Flat 3". In fact, the house had been turned into a boarding house for rich, or fairly rich, theatricals.

This has always been a tradition in Glasgow. The very rich go to hotels, but the rich are still careful of their money and they go, if they can find them, to the traditional theatrical digs. It's important, because hotels don't always realise the special needs of the theatrical profession – to lie in late in the morning, to ask for meals at unusual hours, but most important of all, to have a good, hot meal when they come back from the theatre. And that can be pretty late.

The result is that most landladies of theatrical digs are former music hall and pantomime artists. They cater for the "legitimate" theatre too, of course, but they look for the common touch.

The House on the Hill was now owned by a former pantomime principal boy, Coral McKenzie. Ever since she opened the place she had done well. Hotels, she reflected, were pricing themselves out of the market. She provided good accommodation, but also a kitchen in each flat so that you could make your own meals. Between stage, film and television people she was in constant business. Her only trouble was a nagging desire to return to the stage. She was, after all, only in her mid thirties, was still quite good-looking and had kept her trim figure. But there weren't so many jobs for pantomime principal boys nowadays and she reckoned she was lucky in her present position.

Coral was waiting for a V.I.P. – none other than the great Robbie Kerr, the best-known of the Scots comics and famous for his pantomime dame portrayals. She knew, from experience, that he would be difficult. Top Scots comics were usually difficult, not because they were really difficult people, but because they realised that, as the star of the pantomime, they had a certain reputation to keep up.

Coral glanced around the hall, tastefully decorated with theatrical and other entertainment posters. She looked approvingly at the poster she had just tacked up near the telephone, the best place for people to see it. In big letters at the top it advertised that Robbie Kerr was appearing in *Aladdin* at the King's Theatre, and there was a picture of him on the bill to prove it. The secondary stars were featured, also in photographs, a bit below. Coral frowned slightly as she saw that they were Dicky Viner, who was alleged to be an up-and-coming English comedian, and somebody called Cindy. Cindy? Ah, yes. Coral recalled that Cindy was a pop singer. She felt that pop singers were a drug on the market, but this girl might be an exception. Then her eye fell on the name Julia Jessup, still a principal boy when Coral had prematurely retired. That was Robbie Kerr's long-time "friend". Coral thought of the luxury flat on the ground floor which Robbie and Julia were, as usual, sharing together.

Ah, well, it was none of her business – though sometimes she wished it was. She heard the sound of a taxi arriving outside, looked in the hall mirror to make sure she was perfect, and went to open the door. There was Robbie Kerr, standing aloof and impatient, while Julia paid the taxi-driver. Robbie, masterful as ever, marched up the steps while Julia struggled with two large suitcases.

"Well, now!" cried Coral in welcome. "So here we are again."

Robbie ignored her. He looked back to see what was keeping Julia. "I must say," said Coral, "it's grand to have you both staying here again." Robbie walked into the hall and Julia started struggling up the stairs with the cases. Coral went down to help her and the two women exchanged a glance and a small smile which showed that they realised that Robbie had not changed.

In the hall Robbie Kerr was carefully measuring the size of his name with those of the others on the *Aladdin* bill. "I've had your flat done right through," said Coral. "I'm sure you'll like it." Robbie, satisfied that the billing was in order with his contract, looked at Coral but didn't utter a word. Coral gave him a couple of keys and asked, "So how long will you be running this year?" Still no reply from the magnificent Robbie, who was trying out the keys. Julia picked up the two big cases and replied, "Eleven and a half weeks – one hundred and fifteen performances."

Coral gave Julia what she thought was a compassionate smile. "You sound weary already," she said. Julia tottered into the flat with the heavy cases.

* * *

Robbie Kerr, star comic, always reserved his energies for the stage. But he could not abide lack of energy in other people. He'd looked round the new decor of the flat and tolerated it. He shouted, "We're due in the theatre in just under the hour, Julia."

"Coming," said Julia, lugging a case. Coral followed her with the other case. She was determined to make her mark with Robbie.

"I'll be there on the first night as usual," she said. "So mind you both be good."

"Specially for you, we'll try," Robbie's voice was sarcastic. "The rest of the run we'll be our usual boring selves." He suddenly looked at Coral. "Anyone else staying here – from the cast, I mean?"

"Mr. Viner," said Coral and, as Robbie scowled, "He's stayed here before, you know. And a new girl – new to me, anyway, though I have seen her on the box. Just the one name – Cindy." She looked a little nervously at Robbie. "It always makes me feel they have something to hide – people with just one name."

"She has," Robbie curled his lip. "An awesome lack of talent."

"She did once have a song at number one in the hit parade," said Julia placatingly.

"Aye, once," Robbie returned with scorn. "And how long ago? Since when was that a recommendation of anything? You coming or are you not?"

As Robbie went into the sitting room, Julia said quietly to Coral, "He's on edge – they've put three new dances in since he played it two years ago, so now they're looking for cuts."

"Don't you fret, Mr. Kerr," cried Coral after the disappearing Robbie. "They'd not dare to cut *any* of your material."

Robbie turned round and glared at them. They followed him into the flat and the great comedian said, "Try and convince our director of that. To hear him you'd think

I'd been dead for years. Tits, bums and noise – that's all they care about these days."

"It'll all work out," said Julia. "Wait and see."

"Wait and see won't help the notices!" Robbie was almost shouting. "And what the hell do I have to 'wait and see' for anyway? I tell them and I tell them, year in and year out, 'Familiarity breeds box office. Stick to tradition and you can't fail.' But no – every year the same old story. Some jumped up pansy with a degree in drama and not much else knows best. One of these days they'll wake up and find that pantomime is dead, and *they'll* have killed it."

Julia protested, "We've a twelve-week season and hardly a seat not sold before we open."

Robbie shook his head. "Aye, that's this year. There was a time when it would have been sixteen weeks – twenty, even."

"Even so," said Julia, "you'll survive."

"Damn right I will," snorted Robbie.

As if on cue, there was a tap on the door and the second comic, Dickie Viner, followed by the starry-eyed Cindy, edged in. Robbie Kerr looked at them suspiciously. Had they been listening at the door? "How long have you been out there?" he demanded.

"Just this second arrived," said Dickie quickly, for he had been listening at the door. "This is Cindy."

Coral appraised the couple with some reserve. She knew that Dickie Viner was the randy type, and she saw that Cindy was rather older than the blossoming pop-singer she expected. "Arrived together, did you?" she asked.

"Now, now," Dickie gave one of his famous big laughs – at least he thought they were famous, "None of your Presbyterian prudity. Cindy and I are just good friends."

Cindy gave Coral her sweetest smile. "It's kind of you to let me have a flat, Mrs. McKenzie."

"Just Coral, love," said Coral. "It's bad enough being a widow without being reminded all the time."

"Well, if you'd like to cough up with the keys," said Dickie brightly, "Cindy and I can go and explore our home from home." He turned to Robbie. "I've ordered a cab for the theatre in about five minutes. Like to share?"

"Fine by me," said Robbie shortly.

"Dutch treat," Dickie made the point clear.

"Of course," said Robbie, and watched them leave. Coral shook her head and shrugged.

"One day," Robbie said darkly, "he'll be reading some little tart's true confessions and find he's one of them!"

"He's so indiscreet with it!" Coral commented.

"Discretion is the better part of not being found out," uttered Robbie rather pompously. "And he should have learned that at his age."

"And she's no chicken," Coral shook her head. "Is she any good?"

Robbie shook his head in turn. "She'd do if she'd get on with it instead of giving us a medley of her only hit. I keep telling her – rub the bloody lamp and get on with it!"

"She *is* the principal boy," protested Julia.

Robbie, fond of snorting, snorted again. "Any little scrubber out of the chorus would do as well. They should have had you! My old man always used to say, 'Watch out for the principal boy – she can steal the show, given half a chance'." He turned to Coral. "That's why I always like to have Julia. Knows her place and her limitations. But would they listen this year? Would they hell!"

Outside a taxi horn sounded twice. Dickie Viner stuck his head round the door. He had a gift for being in the right place at the right time. "All aboard for the Skylark," he shouted gaily.

"Well, let's get it over and done with," said Robbie, and led the way out to the taxi.

Coral followed with Julia. "He *is* upset, isn't he?" she said.

"Just scared, that's all," answered Julia. "It's the same every year."

"Him, scared?" Coral was almost shocked. "You'd think after all his years in the business –"

Robbie's stentorian voice came from outside. "For God's sake, Julia!"

Coral followed Julia on to the steps of the house. She waved them off. The expression on her face showed that, stage temperament or not, she'd have liked to be going with them.

The four of them arrived at the King's Theatre and went through the stage door. Julia immediately seized a heavy skip and started to manoeuvre it through Dressing Room Number 1 into the communicating Number 2. Dickie and Cindy looked on with interest. Robbie sat in an easy chair and looked round his dressing room to make sure that the whisky was there. It was and he poured out a drink for himself.

In came Peter Proud, the pantomime producer. "Hi, Peter," shouted Dickie. "And how's the great director?"

Peter gave a limp-wristed flap of the hand. "Harrassed yet hopeful," he ululated and then saw Julia struggling with the skip. "Here, love, I'll give you a hand with that." He took one end of the skip and helped Julia into the Number 2 dressing room, which was packed with Robbie's wigs, dresses and props for the pantomime.

As he came back with Julia, he said to Robbie, "You know about the Press do?"

Julia said quickly, "Thanks, but Robbie can't. His back, you know?"

Robbie disregarded her. "What Press call?" he demanded.

"Oh, goody," cried Cindy. "Will there be photographers?"

"If they say not," said Robbie sourly, "there will be. And if they say there will be, you'll not see a camera in sight."

"It's to be quite a big do," said Peter Proud placatingly. "Costumes, open air reception –"

"In December?" interrupted Robbie incredulously.

"Ours is not to reason why," said Peter.

"Well, I'll be staying indoors," said Robbie positively. "I'll talk with old Wallie, the best theatrical reporter in Glasgow."

"Wallie's retired," said Peter. "There's a new chap in the job – Paul McGregor."

"McGregor? There used to be an editor –"

"This is the son," explained the director.

Dickie Viner broke in. "So what if it rains tomorrow?"

"We all move indoors," said Peter smoothly. "We're having the reception on the terrace outside Coral McKenzie's house and she'll be doing the honours."

Dickie brayed the laugh which signalled a joke. "That's neat! We can fall straight out of bed and into the champagne."

"Why wasn't I told?" frowned Robbie.

"I'm telling you now, aren't I?" said Peter. "Only just heard myself."

"Waste of time anyway," carolled Cindy. "According to the box office there's hardly any seats left for the entire season."

Robbie permitted himself a slight grin. "And that's a better fairy story than we've got in the script!"

"You don't believe it?" asked Cindy.

"When do they ever say anything else?"

"I'm sure we'll do well this year," stated Cindy.

"And what makes you so sure?" asked Robbie.

Cindy preened herself. "My agent says I'm a very big draw."

Robbie Kerr's mouth fell open. For once he was speechless.

* * *

Whisky glass in hand, Robbie Kerr stood at the window looking out at the somewhat bizarre 'reception'. The park was shrouded in mist. On the terrace were most of the cast in their pantomime costumes. He hoped that the goose pimples on the dancing girls wouldn't show in the pictures – if there were any pictures. There was Julia in one of her skimpy costumes, looking blue with cold but still smiling bravely. The photographers seemed to be concentrating on Dickie Viner and Cindy. They must have heard about the 'romance'. The whole thing was a farce, decided Robbie.

He turned as a young man entered the drawing room. He introduced himself as Paul McGregor, successor to Robbie's old newspaper friend.

"You're to take over from Wallie Clune?" asked Robbie.

"He'll be a hard man to follow," admitted McGregor.

"So where have you been hiding yourself?"

"London."

"London, eh?" said Robbie. "Why've you come back?"

"Why do you stay?" riposted McGregor, and Robbie actually smiled.

They sat down on either side of the fire. After some questions and answers McGregor got down to what was clearly the reason for the interview. "So what about next year?" he asked.

"Let's get this show on the road first," said Robbie, "and then worry about next year."

McGregor looked at his notebook. "According to our normal tradition," he said cautiously, "you should be appearing in Edinburgh again."

"I expect so – why?"

McGregor looked at his notebook. "Oh, nothing – just rumours."

"What rumours?"

"We hear things on newspapers," said McGregor. "I expect you know that. There's something going on – I can't put my finger on it."

Julia entered, shivering in her costume and got as close to the fire as she could without interrupting them. McGregor plunged on. "Do you suppose there's a chance they might not ask you to play the Dame next year, Mr. Kerr?"

Robbie looked straight at him. "What have you heard?"

"Nothing definite, you understand," said McGregor nervously. He wondered at once if he should have avoided this subject.

"But there's no smoke without fire," said Robbie. "Is that it?" He heard people in the hall and deliberately raised his voice. "It's politics, McGregor. That's all anything is these days – politics."

Peter Proud came in, followed by one of the head executives in the theatre, Mr. Macleod. Robbie pretended not to notice their arrival and in the same loud voice said, "They're all very good at destroying – very keen to tear things down. Not so good when it comes to the building up again."

Peter Proud broke in uneasily. "Everything all right, Robbie?"

"An excuse is what they're after?" Robbie asked the empty air. "I've worked thirty years and more to get where I am and some snotty-nosed, pen-pushing little civil servant can wipe it all out at a stroke!"

"Got to crack the whip, I'm afraid," said Peter Proud. "We've a dress rehearsal and a first night to think of, Mr. McGregor. And if this party takes a hold, no one'll be fit for anything."

"Meaning me, I suppose?" glared Robbie.

Julia intervened. "Would you excuse us, gentlemen? We have to get ready for rehearsal."

The two men looked anxiously towards Robbie but went back to the party in the hall.

"Get Laurie," Robbie ordered Julia. "He's got to handle this."

Julia went out to the telephone in the hall, avoiding the people who were still enjoying the party. Robbie Kerr poured himself another big dram of whisky.

After a minute or so Julia came back. "Laurie's in Aberdeen," she reported.

"What kind of an agent is he? I need him here."

"Robbie." said Julia softly, "this is Laurie Cameron's busiest time – Christmas."

"And I'm his busiest client all the year round!" Robbie was shouting again. "What's he doing in Aberdeen anyway? They don't open until next week."

"They've lost their principal boy," explained Julia.

"That's careless!"

"Mary McNee," Julia was still explaining.

"Ah! We've all been trying to lose her for long enough. How did they manage it?"

Julia shrugged. "They've booked some English comic – and he uses a dog in his act."

"So?"

"It's got second billing, over Mary, and in bigger print."

Robbie was shocked. "A dog?" he repeated. "But

Aberdeen is Mary's home town. She'll be a laughing stock." He brooded a bit.

"They billed a dog over Mary McNee in her home town?" Robbie couldn't get over it. "What's the panto?"

"Dick Whittington."

"And his *dog*?"

Julia laughed. Robbie reproved her. "It's not funny. They can do it to Mary this year and they can do it to us the next. So what am I talking about? Next year! If McGregor's right there's not going to be a next year – not for me anyway."

"We'd better go," urged Julia. "Peter wants to talk cuts before the rehearsal this afternoon." She took the empty glass from Robbie's hand.

* * *

Peter Proud was having a terrible time with his temperamental stars. After a furious scene with Dickie Viner and Cindy, he went into Robbie's dressing room and explained that cuts still had to be made.

Robbie said flatly, "I'm not chopping and changing my act at this stage."

"It's only a dress rehearsal this afternoon," pleaded Peter. "Just one routine? One clean cut?"

Robbie changed his tone. "I'm an old man, don't you see? I'd get confused."

"Ten Green Bottles?" suggested the producer nervously.

"That stays," Robbie was himself again. "I've paid good money for an entirely new routine."

"It's very long," protested Peter.

"So what do you suggest? Five Green Bottles?" Robbie glared at him. "I'm contracted to play *my* Widow Twankey. Not yours, some half-wit scribbler's or anybody else's. I'll not short-change my audience for anyone. Now, if you'll excuse me, I've to check my props before the rehearsal – including my Ten Green Bottles." He walked into Julia's dressing room as Julia came out of it. It was obvious that she had heard the exchanges between Robbie and Peter. She patted Peter on the shoulder and said softly, "Don't worry, love, we've been in this bag before, you know. We'll just top and tail a bit, put the foot down and you'll save at least five minutes by tonight." Peter smiled at her gratefully.

And Julia was right, although the dress rehearsal was the usual shambles. It's not surprising that the words, 'It'll be all right on the night,' have passed into current usage. If Robbie had been tense before, he was much worse now, and taking his nervousness out on her. He rushed into his dressing room where Julia was waiting with his next costume, wig and an enormous bead necklace all ready.

As he started to tear off the dress he was wearing, she unzipped him down the back. "What's next?" shouted Robbie, wild-eyed and sweating.

"Emperor's Garden, the Love Duet. Then the Bead Dance."

"I know what I bloody *do*!" Robbie cried. "What do I wear?"

"It's all here," soothed Julia. "And your thigh boots and orange wig are in the quick change room off left. I'll be there waiting when you come off."

"You'd bloody better be!" He looked at her. "Those tights of yours need darning."

Julia looked ruefully at her legs. "They've been darned so often, there's no 'tight' left." As Robbie looked daggers at her, she said, "All right, all right, I'll do it before I go on. I have time."

"So I'm glad one of us has!" With Julia's assistance Robbie's change was almost completed. He suddenly became human again. "How's it going do you think?" he asked.

"They love you – and you know it."

He grabbed the beads and dashed out.

But all bad things, even pantomime dress rehearsals, come to an end. Back in their own clothes, actors, dancers and some of the stage crew were drinking wine, thoughtfully provided by the management. Peter Proud was talking to the important Macleod. "It was still a shade over long, don't you think?" he said with appropriate modesty.

"Stop worrying, Peter," said Macleod. "You did a grand job. You always do." There was a burst of applause when Robbie Kerr, immaculate as usual, walked on to the stage with Julia.

Macleod leaned close to Peter. "Is tonight the right time, do you think?" he asked.

"I'd wait," said Peter, just as softly.

"How do you think he'll react?"

Peter shrugged. "The man's a genius – so he says. What mere mortal can predict a mind like his?"

Around Robbie there was much handshaking, backslapping and offers of drink. Laurie Cameron, the agent, stood watching the scene along with Dickie Viner, Cindy and Coral. "Excuse me," he said to them and moved towards Robbie.

"Sure," said Dickie in a loud alcoholic voice. "Go on and protect your ten per cent. For handling a turd like him I'd want at least ninety."

Robbie's head lifted. It was obvious that he had heard Viner's remark. Laurie tried to cover up by saying, "Wonderful, Robbie – fabulous. Dare I say better than ever?"

Robbie said quietly, "So what about Edinburgh next year? Was that reporter right or not?"

Laurie gave a big smile for the benefit of anyone who

was watching them. He replied equally soft, "I've tried, but no joy. Something's cooking but they're not telling. Still, it's early days. I'm sure you're worrying for nothing."

"You can afford to be sure," Robbie said. "You only stand to lose *ten* per cent."

"There's more than money between us, I hope, Robbie!"

"Not a lot," Robbie's eyes were glittering. "Lose me that contract and there won't even be that." He turned to Julia irritably. "Are you getting me another drink or not?"

Julia kept her cool. "What about you, Laurie?" she asked the agent.

"Thanks, Julia," said Laurie, handing her his glass. "And congratulations. Still the best pair of legs in the business."

"And the oldest pair of tights!" smiled Julia.

As Laurie watched Julia go for the drinks he said, "You're a lucky man, Robbie. Why don't you marry the girl? She's a first-rater."

"I know that," said Robbie. "I trained her. She was a tuppeny-ha'penny hoofer in the back row when I picked her out."

Coral, seeing Julia making for the bar, walked quickly towards Robbie. He was saying, "She can always go back to it if she's so minded." He saw Coral's approach and raised his voice. "Or pack it all in and start running love-nests for clapped out comedians."

"Now, now, Mr. Kerr," cried Coral archly, "remember what the pot called the kettle."

"I'm not a married man," said Robbie.

"And there's no need to tell *me* that! You were wonderful tonight, simply wonderful."

Dickie Viner, getting steadily drunker, was talking to the producer. "Maybe you're right, Peter," he slurred.

"He can make an exit better than anyone you know. The trouble is he doesn't make them soon enough and often enough."

Coral had succeeded in getting the conversation in her direction. She looked directly at Laurie Cameron and said, "I still dream of making a come-back. If only I can find the right agent. Or do you think it's too late, Mr. Cameron?"

"It's never too late for talent," said Laurie. He'd had this kind of conversation before.

Robbie interrupted, "Why don't we drink up and go back to the house? Have a private party where we know the natives are friendly?"

Julia came back with the drinks. Robbie kept looking over at the group of executives. What mischief were they planning? He thought it might be a good idea to get drunk that night.

And, by the time the four of them had got back to the flat in the House on the Hill, Robbie was well on the way to getting drunk. They were still talking about their one-and-only subject, the stage, when they heard the front door slam.

"Ah!" said Robbie. "The love-birds stagger back to their nest at last!"

There was a knock on the door and Laurie went to open it. In weaved Dickie Viner, leaning heavily on the supporting Cindy. As he saw Laurie, Viner shouted, "Ah, Mr. Ten-per-cent himself!"

"Plus VAT," said Laurie agreeably.

Julia smiled at Dickie. "You look as if you've had a good time," she said.

"And why not?" demanded Dickie, almost truculently.

Robbie looked at him. "I wouldn't have thought you'd a lot to celebrate."

"I got my laughs!" protested Dickie.

"And my agent loved my numbers," put in Cindy.

Dickie couldn't wait to tell his news. "And I," he said, "had a most profitable little chat with Macleod. They're mounting a fabulous, brand new production of *Humpty-Dumpty* next year. In Edinburgh – and guess who'll be the star of the show!"

He performed an elaborate stage bow and nearly fell on the floor. Robbie Kerr stared at him incredulously.

"Hump-er-ty Dump-er-ty, old boy," grinned Dickie.

"Did Macleod not mention me at all?" said Robbie sharply.

"Sorry, chum. Your name didn't come up once."

Cindy looked at Dickie in surprise. She was about to speak, but a disturbed Robbie broke in. "They can't do that. Not without me!"

Dickie waved his hands expansively. "They can do anything they choose to do."

Robbie turned to his agent. "My Queen Gizzinta is famous. They can't do that."

"Looks like they're going to have a damn good try. Goodnight, your Majesty." Dickie attempted another bow and would have fallen if Cindy hadn't grabbed him. She pushed him to the door and they heard her trying to get him upstairs.

Laurie had closed the door and now he turned to Robbie. "I'll talk to Macleod in the morning," he said. "It must be a mistake. Or maybe that joker's just winding you up."

"Get out!" roared Robbie. "Call yourself an agent? Where are you when you're needed? Nowhere. Poncing about in Aberdeen. They only do a five week run."

"We'll talk in the morning," soothed Laurie.

"Don't bother. You're fired – sacked – finished – kaput. Understand?"

"I don't think you mean that, Robbie."

"Get out!" roared Robbie again. "Now – straight away. I never want to see your creepy little face again. And I *do* mean that."

Laurie looked at Julia with raised eyebrows. As Robbie walked rather uncertainly into the bedroom, Julia said quietly, "You'd better go, Laurie. I'll be all right. And you, Coral, if you don't mind."

Coral had been an astonished observer of the whole scene. "Well," she said, "talk about Beauty and the Beast!"

They went out. Julia went to the bedroom door. "That was a pretty rotten thing to do," she said. "You have to give him six months notice anyway."

Robbie reappeared. "And what've they done to me?" he demanded. "You call that fragrant."

"If I had your enemies, I'd hang on to my friends. Even if Dickie's telling the truth, it's not Laurie's fault."

"So whose fault is it?" asked Robbie. "Mine?" He picked up the whisky bottle.

"Don't drink any more, Bobby – not tonight," pleaded Julia.

Robbie poured himself a large dram as Julia went into the bedroom.

He swallowed the whisky in one go, and poured himself another. All of a sudden he shouted at the bedroom door, "You heard the audience – they loved me. Same as they always have. It's not *me* they don't want. The whole thing is deliberate. How many times have I done Humpty Dumpty? A whole lifetime of Humpty Dumpties and what do they give me in return? Nothing. There's no love, no loyalty, nothing – not any more."

He went to the bedroom door and threw it open. Julia was half undressed and looking frightened at Robbie's onslaught. "But maybe it's not me that they don't want," he said bitterly.

"And what does that mean?" asked Julia, trying to put a brave front on it.

The drunken Robbie wavered, pulled himself together and said harshly, "A bit long in the tooth for it, aren't you? A bit saggy and baggy to be prancing around in split skirts and torn fish-nets. Maybe it's you they don't want. Maybe they've found out about us."

Julia had recovered her composure. "For heaven's sake," she said, "Everyone's known for years."

"Not the kids, but nowadays they grow up fast. Maybe that's what they're laughing at – you and me – we're just a dirty joke to them. Twankey shacked up with Aladdin – Crusoe in the kip with his mum. Adds a new dimension, doesn't it? Maybe that's why Macleod didn't want you for principal boy this year. Look at you! I mean, who could stand it?"

Julia was in tears and had started to dress again. She pushed past him into the sitting room. Robbie followed her. "That's right," he was still shouting. "Walk out on me. Do me a favour. I'll call Laurie first thing and tell him I'm free – free to play Gizzinta, without wrapping you around the management's neck. That'll fix it. You'll see."

Julia was dressed now and she ran out of the sitting room. Robbie poured himself yet another whisky. "Flabby, dabby old slag," he called after her.

He slumped in his armchair, taking frequent gulps of whisky. Suddenly the door opened and Coral came in. She had changed into a house-coat and slippers.

"So what the hell do you want?" asked Robbie.

"I thought perhaps you'd like some company," said Coral. "I know how you hate being on your own."

"I'll manage," Robbie dismissed her.

"But what if she doesn't come back?" Robbie looked at Coral blankly and she quickly added, "You'll need someone – at home, in the theatre. And I make a good principal boy. I've got my press cuttings to prove it."

As Robbie tried to focus on the proposition, Coral came forward to sit beside him. She brought the whisky bottle with her and poured out another dram. He realised that her house-coat was open to the waist. Was she the answer? He took another drink and reached out towards her.

* * *

Robbie Kerr always thought he was right in everything he did. But he was slightly worried about his first night aftermath. He knew he'd had a row with Julia and she'd walked out. But tonight, in his dressing room, he heard her moving about in her own room. He'd tried the door handle and found that Julia had locked it. Well, he'd been drunk before and she always forgave him. The thing that really worried him was that he could hear a muted conversation through the door. Who was talking to Julia and what were they saying?

It was his agent who was in Julia's dressing room. "You realise," said Laurie, "that if you leave him for good, he'll be crippled."

"He already is emotionally," replied Julia, "and I'm tired of being his crutch."

Laurie looked directly at her. "Have you told him yet?"

"He told me, remember?" said Julia bitterly.

Laurie said, "That was last night. First night hysteria and all that."

There was a knock on the dividing door. Laurie rose to open it. "Leave it," said Julia. Laurie stopped. He turned to Julia with a worried look when Robbie's voice came from the other side. "Julia!" he shouted. Julia said not a word. There was the sound of a curse behind the door, and in a few seconds Robbie marched in from the corridor, half ready for the next scene and wigless. He saw Laurie but ignored him. "What the hell do you think you're playing at?" he shouted at Julia.

She was sitting at her mirror and didn't look round. "Just patching up the saggy old bag a bit, that's all," she shrugged. "A few bits of sellotape, a touch of polyfilla, and you can work wonders."

"I can't find the right wig."

"It's in there somewhere," said Julia off-handedly.

Robbie was still shouting. "I can't find *anything*. That's *your* job."

This time Julia looked at him. "Not any more," she said. "If you'll excuse me, Mr. Kerr, and close the door as you go – I'm still only half renovated."

Robbie was speechless. He turned and went out, slamming the door. Julia looked at Laurie, who was obviously miserable about the turn of events. "Such a graceful apology, did you notice?"

When the pantomime started, Julia kept out of Robbie's way. Peter Proud stood in the wings aghast, as his chief comic seemed to be going to pieces. The newspaper critics looked across the aisle at each other in surprise. What had happened to Robbie Kerr? He was one comedian who always seemed to be in complete control of his material. Those nearest the stage could see that, underneath the dame make-up, Robbie Kerr seemed a very uncertain man.

The show went on. Cindy was in song, the dancers were in the wings ready for their next appearance, and Robbie Kerr was struggling to fasten the giant string of beads round his neck. The string broke and the beads scattered among the feet of the dancers. Robbie scrabbled on the floor, trying to retrieve the beads. The dancers made no attempt to move or to help him. Julia came through for her next appearance and saw Robbie on his knees. Her impulse was to turn away, but she relented, went towards him and said, "Bobby –"

He looked up at her from the floor, tears of panic in his eyes, and held out a small handful of the beads towards her.

"That's the wrong hat," said Julia. "You can't do your twirly dance in that, you'll strangle yourself. And there's a spare necklace in your big jewel case.

Robbie got to his feet and Julia turned away from him. He started for his dressing room to find the spare necklace. Julia suddenly turned round and called after him, "It's the pork pie hat."

Cindy was still singing and the dancers looked surprised at the interruption. Julia saw the stage manager making for her and prepared for a telling-off.

At the interval Peter Proud came to Julia's dressing room. "Please, love," he pleaded. "He's gone to pieces – ruined the act one finale. You've got to sort him out for the second half."

Julia shook her head. "I'm not his nurse, his dresser – I'm not his wife. He's not my problem."

"Think of the audience – those poor kiddies –"

"Spare me the bleeding hearts, Peter," said Julia.

"Please!"

Julia looked at Peter, then rose and unlocked the dividing door. She saw Robbie slumped at the dressing table, staring into the mirror at the face of an old, tired, defeated man. "Come on, then, Bobby," she said to him. "Time for beginners."

"I can't," moaned Robbie. "Not again. I can't go out there again."

Julia started to sort out his next costume and the necessary props. "Rubbish," she said strongly. "An old pro like you? Point yourself at the limelight and switch to automatic pilot."

"I just," he swallowed. "I just fell apart out there."

"So, you made a bad start," Julia's voice had an authoritative ring. "Now's the time to go out there and knock 'em dead. Macleod's out front – and God knows who else."

"Macleod?" repeated Robbie. The miserable look was wiped off his face. Julia saw her chance. "Come on," she urged. "You can still show them a trick or two, can't you?"

She held out his next dress. Robbie rose with a new light in his eye. Yes, he would show them.

The second half of *Aladdin* was a revelation to those who had wondered what was wrong with Robbie Kerr. He was the same old swaggering dame, master of the stage. At the end of the show his entrance down the traditional palace steps was greeted with an ovation.

And, when they were back in their dressing rooms, Julia told Robbie that she wanted to dissolve their partnership.

"So that's it, then?" said Robbie.

Julia was firm. "It's what I want and I think it's what you want, really."

"So what will you do?"

"Laurie's working on it now," said Julia.

There was the sound of laughter from the corridor. Through the dressing room door they could see Dickie Viner, Macleod, Cindy, Peter Proud and a couple of strangers passing along.

"Will you just listen to them?" said Robbie. "What do they know about anything?" He was in the depths again. "I'm too tired to be messed around," he said, "and there's an end to it."

There was a tap on Julia's door and Laurie Cameron came in with young McGregor. Robbie broke the awkward pause by saying, "I'll leave you and your agent to discuss things." He turned to McGregor and said, "If you've a minute, I've something that might interest you." He went into his own room. McGregor hesitated for a moment, then followed him. The dividing door closed.

Laurie, not quite as miserable as he had been, said, "Well, you're all set. You go to Aberdeen tomorrow. They rehearse you on Saturday and Sunday and you open on the Monday."

"And the billing?"

"Still under that bloody dog, I'm afraid," said Laurie. "But the money's good to compensate."

"Mary McNee won't change her mind?" Julia asked.

"Given half a chance she might. But she's blown it."

"Come on," said Julia, "I'll buy you a drink to celebrate."

In Robbie's dressing room the great dame was talking to McGregor.

"Your grandfather and my father were good friends. So I've decided to let you be the first to know. I've decided to retire from pantomime. This engagement will mark my last appearance as the Dame. Is that news or not?"

"Well, yes, but–" started McGregor and then asked, "I can print that?"

Robbie nodded and McGregor got out his notebook. "Perhaps you'd like to give me a resumé of your life – your career. I'll maybe get a feature out of it."

"Like an obituary, you mean?" He saw McGregor was embarrassed and said, "Don't worry. I can take a joke as well as tell one. Now, where would you like to start – before or after the Flood?"

Which was all very well, but Robbie soon learned that Julia was in earnest. She told him she was to be the principal boy in Aberdeen.

"And what about me?" he asked her. I'd have gone under tonight. Without you, I mean."

"I'm sure Coral will soon learn the ropes. After all, she's an old pro."

"She's an old bag," said Robbie in his charming way.

"That's not what you seemed to think last night," said Julia. "After I'd had a good cry on Cindy's shoulder, I came back down here – thinking you'd be asleep. You weren't. And I think Coral knew exactly what she was doing."

Robbie thought he'd better change the subject. "And what about you?" he asked. "After Aberdeen."

"We finish a week earlier than you do," said Julia. "After that . . . maybe find a fella. Get married. I mean, really married, settle down." She collected her case, went to the door and asked, "Shall I tell Coral?"

"Tell her what?" said Robbie, bemused.

"To come through. You can make a start teaching her your routines." She walked out. Robbie poured himself another drink.

* * *

The news of Robbie Kerr's retirement was out. It had caused quite a sensation in the theatre. Peter Proud and the enigmatic Macleod came into Robbie's dressing room where Coral, now in Julia's role, was helping him into his entrance costume. Peter explained that a big presentation ceremony had been planned for Robbie at the end of the run.

"Just to say goodbye to an old has-been?" enquired Robbie bitterly.

Macleod broke in. "To say goodbye to a tradition, a golden age. It's a sad passing for the theatre here in Scotland, Robbie. We're determined to mark the occasion in the proper manner."

Peter indicated the evening paper lying on the dressing table. "Since this appeared this afternoon," he said, "the box office telephones haven't stopped. Everybody wants to see you one last time."

"Then they'll be disappointed," said Robbie.

Macleod looked at him. "We could extend the run, maybe –"

"No," said Robbie. Laurie Cameron came in with an evening paper. "And what do you want?" demanded Robbie. "Come to mourn for your ten per cent."

"Money I can always find," replied Laurie. "Genius is more of a problem. I've just seen Julia off. She said to tell you, it seemed a miserable way to wave goodbye to twenty-five years. And to wish you luck in your retirement."

Robbie looked as if he hadn't heard a word. Coral was doing her best to do what Julia had told her to do. "Will you stop messing me about, woman?" snarled Robbie.

"Sorry," said Coral and retired to what had been Julia's room. The men talked about Robbie's farewell party, but Robbie paid little attention. When they left, Coral came back into the dressing room with another dress for Robbie. He said sourly, "In the routines, if you can't remember the steps, at least look as though you're trying."

"I'm nervous," Coral confessed. "It's been such a long time."

"Talent's like riding a bike," pontificated Robbie. "You never forget. And smile, for God's sake. Your face would trip a cat."

"I'm sorry," said Coral, then added, "The party – will I be there? With you, I mean?"

Unlike his customary brash style, Robbie hesitated. "We'll see. We've a few weeks to go yet."

But, when it came to the night of the farewell party, Robbie was glad to have Coral with him. He had not heard a single word from Julia, but he had been told that she had made a great success as the principal boy in *Dick Whittington* in Aberdeen. He looked round the stage, still set for the palace walk down scene. He registered that the affair was being done in style, with decorations, champagne and a long buffet table. A television crew were filming the proceedings. There were even several people in full evening dress. Robbie turned his attention to the speech which Macleod was making. He noted that the grey eminence was holding a baby grandfather clock.

"We'll all miss you, Robbie," Macleod was saying. "Christmas time will not be the same. And, as for next year – well, it's an open secret now – we had hoped to pay special tribute in our new production of *Humpty Dumpty*." Robbie's eyes widened as Macleod went on, "We'd hoped to bill you as what I'm sure all present will agree that you are –" he turned the clock towards Robbie so that the comic could read the inscription.

"The World's Greatest Dame," read out Macleod. "With our thanks, gratitude and love."

The audience burst into applause. Robbie took the clock and looked stunned. He didn't see Julia and Laurie Cameron come in at the back of the stage. Once he collected himself, he started on the sort of speech he'd been making for most of his life. His every gag was greeted rapturously and then he suddenly became serious.

"Now I'm not going to make a speech," he said and got the usual laugh. "But there are one or two things that need to be said. You all of you know Julia – Julia Jessup, my partner of twenty-four years." The crowd were suddenly silent. "Well, Julia's not here. After all that time of working without complaint and a great deal to complain about in my shadow, she's moved on to seek her own place in the sun. I don't blame her, and I wish her well. Of all my mistakes I can think of no other that I made so consistently and for so long. Perhaps if I'd married her when we first met, our partnership might not have been so easily broken. If any of you should run into her, give her my love – and tell her that I miss her dearly."

Julia, at the back of the stage, slipped out unnoticed. Robbie, clutching his clock, went out, followed by Coral. He did his best to smile at the back-slappers and good-wishers but all he wanted to do was to get into safety at home – and home meant the House on the Hill.

They went into the flat and Robbie, as he always seemed to be doing these days, poured himself a very big whisky. Coral looked at him nervously.

"So they wanted to bill me as the World's Greatest Dame!" said Robbie. "Father would have admired that."

Coral plucked up courage. "And what happens to me, after the season ends tomorrow?" she asked.

"How the hell should I know?"

"I'd thought, perhaps," Coral ventured, "after the last few weeks, maybe you and me."

Robbie cut her short. "You got what you wanted out of me, didn't you? You're back in the business. Go and whine to your agent, not to me. Good night, Coral."

"Well – if that's how you feel." Corals eyes filled with tears and she left the sitting room.

Robbie poured out yet another drink and walked into the bedroom. His eye fell on a photograph of Julia on the bedside table. He picked up a bottle of sleeping pills and stood there with whisky in one hand and pills in the other. He didn't hear the flat door open behind him.

In came Julia quietly. She put her case down, went to the bedroom and he saw her in the dressing table mirror. He turned round. "So what do you want?" he grated. "Did you forget something?"

"Yes," said Julia.

"How was Aberdeen?" asked Robbie. "Did you find your true love?"

"No," said Julia. "I've come back."

"Just like that?"

Julia smiled. "Just like you will – next year as Dame Spritely. After all, you'd not be the first to make a comeback by public demand."

Robbie put down his whisky and the bottle of pills. "You really think I could?"

"Some of them make a profession out of their farewell appearances."

"That's true," reflected Robbie, walking into the sitting room.

Julia followed him. "I was at the party tonight," she said. "It was quite a speech."

"Well, you know me!" Robbie was himself again. "Make 'em laugh – make 'em cry. It did the trick."

"Yes," said Julia simply. "Yes, it did."

Robbie pointed to the baby grandfather clock. "So what will I do with this bloody thing?"

"Keep it," advised Julia. "Or maybe they'll have it back – save it for your next retirement."

Robbie was startled. "Oh, I know you!" said Julia. "You'll not be able to resist an encore." She paused. "Is it all right, then?"

"Is what all right?"

"Shall I unpack?"

"Suit yourself," shrugged Robbie. He picked up the whisky bottle, changed his mind and put it down again. Julia smiled and went into the bedroom.

Robbie looked at her case, still there on the floor. Suddenly he grabbed the case and carried it in to the bedroom for her.

Julia, already undressing, looked at him and smiled. She knew he'd never change. But now she knew more than that.